PRAISE FOR THE BOOK, "MAGICAL WITH MONSTERS"

Gary, I would like to Thank You for asking me to read your manuscript. Over the years I have known you, I knew you wrote for many sources and created many posts, but did not know you were a gifted author of books. While reading the chapters, it gave me the feeling as if I was in a story, watching the chapters play out. To me, that was amazing!

You have created a book that makes the readers want to know what happens next. This manuscript is fantastic, and you are a great writer!

Terri Francisco-Farrell, Kennewick, WA

When I first started reading Book Six of Imperealisity, "MAGICAL WITH MONSTERS," I felt I was in the Denarian lands.

New things were happening every day. You never knew what to expect From one chapter to the next. It's a spell-binding book.

It's so well written that you feel like you're part of the team helping everyone around you. In all of the books in this series, I have always felt I have been there.

Thank you, Gary Downing, for another winner.

Josephine Davis Three Oaks, Michigan

With new friends joining Marty, Steve, and Bailey, their fantastical adventures continue into the magical Denarian Lands. I've enjoyed learning about these characters and watching them grow into themselves as people, but also in their powers. I'm looking forward to seeing what mystical intrigue awaits them next. This series is well written; I sincerely hope all young readers put this on their read list.

Gary, thank you for allowing me to read your latest manuscript. You have put so much heart into this fantastic world that you have created in your books. Truly magical!

Heather Harris of Kennewick, WA

IMPEREALISITY

MAGICAL WITH MONSTERS
BOOK SIX

Gary Wayne

Library of Congress Control Number: 2023920499
ISBN: Hardcover   979-8-3694-1002-8
                 Softcover   979-8-3694-1001-1
                 eBook   979-8-3694-1000-4

Cover artwork - created by Downing Art Works, assisted by Fiver.

Print information available on the last page.

Rev. date: 11/02/2023

To order additional copies of this book, contact: *Be sure to check out the following websites:*
Xlibris   *www.imperealisity.com*
844-714-8691   *www.imperealisity.us*
www.Xlibris.com
Orders@Xlibris.com
852687

**I dedicte this book to my best friend for over
25 years and my editor**

**MY FRIEND
MARILYN TAYLOR**
A warm heart, a loving
and caring person.
I will miss you

Marilyn Taylor
November 4, 1952 - March 15, 2023

*(Book Six, "MAGICAL WITH MONSTERS," is dedicated
to my best friend, who passed away recently. She was always
the person who loved even the simplest things in life.*

*After moving from California to the Tri-Cities in Washington
State, we found what she needed. A new home with property,
more freedom, and her horse she named "TESS."*

*She loved the places we visited, especially in the Pacific Northwest.
My close friend for over 25 years will be remembered.)*

CONTENTS

INTRODUCTION

In the beginning, there was a land far, far away. Oh, sorry, that was another story. However, I guess you could say it fits as our team of heroes has traveled to a new world called Imperealisity.

Looking back now at how it all began, we could see young adult students attending school, doing things around the home, and having discussions with friends. But look at them now. They are traveling on a distant planet in a horse-drawn wagon, saving lives, helping others, and doing the impossible while even fighting unheard-of creatures and beasts.

At first, it was only visions of what was to come as Bailey told Marty, "I see you with a black-and-white dog." Of course, at that time, he didn't have one. It wasn't long before Steve adopted a small ferret, Bailey adopted a kitten, and Marty found his new protector at the Humane Society, a black-and-white-dog.

Then it was Marty stepping through the opening to a brand-new world. After fighting a beast, Steve told him, "I guess we need to go back with you to protect you." Of course, all three of them laughed at that one. However, it didn't take long before our three heroes with their new protectors faced many new adventures.

They gained powers, pets could change, and soon they were saving lives and traveling to the Denarian Lands.

I hope you have been traveling this path with our team as it seems like many months to get to where they are now. However, returning to Earth with a few who never knew what the future was like, they found it has only been weeks back home.

So far, they have created friendships, saved a god, freed people from slavery, met a king and queen, and lost Steve down a hole in the ground, but it's okay They found him, and they have had adventures you, as a reader, have wished you experienced.

In the last book, you found out about that unexplained power wave that felt like an impact on the planet. You also learned about two new travelers from other realms who are now part of this team. This planet is still far, far away, but you are with this team as they help, respect, care for others, and save lives. You are with them as they find more powers and can even communicate with ghosts.

As we leave our team in Book five, *The Digs*, this is what was taking place.

Near the end of those steps, they found a gate near the top of a mountain. Entering those gates and following a path, they gazed upon a city possibly thousands of years old.

Steve said, "This is cool."

One of the excavation crew looked at Steve, then turned and looked at me and asked, "Cool? I find we could not ask for better weather for this find even in this fog. However, I do have to agree the mist in the air does make it feel cool."

Suddenly it was Tom who spoke up, saying, "When he says it's 'cool,' he means incredible, neat, or merely fantastic. But hey, I was not sure what it meant myself when I first heard that word used a day or two ago."

All of us were standing on what appeared to be an extensive carved-out area of slight variation overlooking the entire city below.

All our team was talking about what we could see from here. Tabby was near me, and she asked me, "How old do you think this place is?"

"I'm not sure," I replied.

Nomi, who was standing next to Jack, said, "Look how those trees have grown through those buildings over all the years."

Jack replied, "Yes, notice how vines and brush are all around and even covering some of those structures."

Bailey said, "I have seen photos of ancient ruins that had trees growing up through buildings like that, but to see it in front of us so we can really walk up to it is entirely different."

Catrina walked over, along with our other mothers, and said, "I would never have imagined all the things we have seen since we have been here. Bones and bodies and old ruins are things we hope to see at home sometime. I mean not so much the bodies but ancient, old things of importance to a culture."

"We understand," Steve said.

"Yes, we do, as we have seen and found some of the most unusual things in this world none of us ever expected to see," I spoke.

Nomi commented, "Well, I think it's time we made our way over to that building that looks like some kind of castle to see what stories it holds."

Jack said, "Everyone needs to be sure of your footing as much of this ground may simply crumble below us."

One of the excavation members who walked up with us spoke out and asked, "Why don't all of you allow me to walk ahead of you just in case?" Then he tossed Mortice a rope and tied the other end around himself just under his arms.

I asked him, "What's your name so I can make sure the people know how to spell your name correctly on your tombstone?"

He turned and looked at me and asked, "Is it going to be a big tombstone?"

I said, "You realize I was just kidding about that."

He broke out laughing, and everyone else did as well. Finally, he exclaimed, "My name is Metzler, John Metzler, and you make sure they spell that correctly." Then he laughed again.

The procession was underway as all of us followed John around fallen trees and huge rocks, under and through brush and debris. As we approached yet another gate, we found this one off its hinges, with one side on the ground. There was an arch over it that almost looked like a crown.

As we looked around, I felt this entire location was something no one could ever find. We could look up, and most of what was over us were vines, tree branches, and little or no sunlight. I was still feeling something strange, and as all of us viewed this place, I expected something just to pop out and grab us.

I could picture being in an airplane and flying over this setting and looking down and only finding a green landscape. I started thinking back to our forest in the Blue Mountains at home with the brush and trees, but our woods were not like this. This place had the weirdest-looking trees, and some of them were growing around some of the buildings.

Everyone was excited about what they saw. At one time, it was a place where people had a community, raised families, and certainly lived in peace. Unfortunately, I am sure very few, if any, people even know this place exists.

John finally saw an opening into one of the more significant buildings. It looked more like a temple with an expansive entry. As we moved into the space, we located what looked to be a walkway. It was over what looked like two floors below. The path we were about to walk on had been created out of metal and stone.

Unfortunately, most of the metal had seen its better days. All of us were slowly walking behind John on that pathway when suddenly John turned and looked at all of us and said, "I am not ready to attempt walking any farther across this."

Nomi said, "I am with you on that one. Let's find a different way to those other buildings."

I looked at that walkway, and Steve and Bailey were both viewing it as well. So I said, "Hey, buddy, whatever you do, please don't breathe hard now."

"Oh, funny. Like my breathing could blow that walkway apart," Steve replied.

Bailey said, "Steve, he may have a valid point." Then she started laughing, and everyone around us did the same.

Many of them were saying things like "Steve, just cover your mouth," "Hold your breath, Steve," and "Oh, that would be a real problem."

"Fine, all of you, please turn around, and let's find a different direction," Steve remarked.

John spoke up and said, "This way might work," and all of us tagged along. As we walked, some people talked about other locations and things they ran into as they searched the areas. One of the men said, "We found beasts living in one area we searched that had lots of overgrowth like this further out west."

Another person spoke and said, "John, be careful. Remember that time we found that nest of snakes was much like this kind of a place."

"Snakes?" We heard Steve ask.

"Oh yes, these kinds of places are loaded with them, so you must keep an eye open. Some of those snakes are so deadly that if a person is bitten, he may not live through the night in most cases."

"Marty, can you heal snakebites?" Steve asked.

"I'm not sure what I can heal, buddy," I replied.

"Great, this is getting scary for me because I really hate snakes. But you healed that scorpion wound on that one man," Steve remarked.

Wanda spoke up and said, "Son, someone here can cure a snakebite, I'm sure, and with all of your own power, I would be surprised if you couldn't do it yourself."

Others were talking about what they viewed ahead of us. The fog was setting back in on us, and visibility was now about twenty feet. Nomi and Mortice yelled at everyone to keep up and join them as they entered a building. I turned and noticed Vanessa, Mom, and the other girls were still chatting away, so I sent Mom a thought saying, *All of you need to catch up. We are losing visibility.*

I noticed she looked around and then spoke to the rest of them. Suddenly all of them collected what they could as they saw the fog closing in and hightailed it in our direction.

As all of us gathered in a group together, we checked to make sure we had everyone. Bailey said, "I sure do feel something strange."

"I have been feeling it for a good amount of time since before we walked through that first gate," I replied.

Vanessa the girls and our mothers were now all feeling something strange as well.

Suddenly, Steve spoke up and asked,
"Could it be that light in that big tower?"

If you have not been reading this series from the first book,
you may feel lost.
If you did not read book five, this has been part of the ending.

However, now that you're here, let's read book six.

Welcome, my friends!

This is Book Six in the Imperealisity Fantasy Series
MAGICAL WITH MONSTERS

CHAPTER 1

What Is Has Been Gone Forever

Walking and listening to Steve, we looked at each other and shook our heads because we could not see any light or tower Steve was referring to.

"What light in what big tower?" Steve's mother, Wanda, asked.

"We need to get rid of this blasted fog somehow and make sure it does not return while all of us are here. I, for one, don't like the idea of the possibility of others being here, knowing all about this place and us being blinded by a cloud," John said.

"I agree with that," a few others commented.

We must have appeared as a group of children. All of us were looking around and heading this way or that, trying to find a window to see what Steve was talking about. It looked just like what Steve said it was, a castle tower. "Well, maybe we have company," Bailey stated.

I looked at Steve, and he just nodded. Suddenly, the wind came up, and the sky was clear. "Thank you," I said.

I heard, "Yes, thank you," "Much better," and Bailey said, "It's sure nice to have our own wind machine."

"Of course," Steve replied. Then we all chuckled.

Steve just gave Bailey a radiant look and said, "Always pleased to help."

Nomi said, "We probably need to keep the noise down as much as possible until we find out who or what is in that tower."

"I think we can get there if we follow that corridor," John said as he pointed toward a hallway.

We explored every room along the way. We even found a few things that impressed us, like the bathhouse area. Not sure how that worked, but it looked like the water used to reach a certain level, and then it flowed out into a large pool area that seemed to have several pipes leading off in all directions. It could have been for warm water in other parts of this building.

Finding another room with large pans and pots reminded us of who lived here. This kitchen was not just for Denarians. It was built and lived in by many different groups of people. Some of them may have been giants, but I would think it was a mix of giants and ordinary-sized people and smaller ones, from the looks of the utensils. More rooms offered us a view of fireplaces, lanterns, and even a few things hanging on the walls that were difficult to make out because of time, weather, and moisture.

Reaching a set of steps that looked like they might be the ones leading up to where we viewed that light, I said, "John, it's time you allowed us to lead just in case we need to use our powers."

He took a step back and said, "That's fine with me because I'm sure no fighter."

Taking the lead, I was followed by Steve, Tom, Art, and Jack, leaving our mothers, Bailey, Vanessa, and the rest of those with us standing on the landing we were now walking away from.

"Wow, this is really creepy," Steve said.

Jack replied, "Steve, I must agree with you on this one as we have no idea what is up there."

Tom said, "I feel whatever it is will not have more power than what is in this small group."

Art said, "I have found I must agree with you."

Climbing what seemed to be forever, we were now standing in a small hallway at the top. It looked like some kind of observation post where soldiers could search and view everything around them. And it was one heck of a view without that fog. The five of us were looking out of each window area, and with that fog gone now, we could see what seemed like a good twenty-five miles easily.

There were a couple of rooms, and one of them had a large door. It was off to one side of the landing. Jack looked at it, walked over, grabbed the lock on the door, and said, "Marty, look at the size of this lock. I can't open this, should we bring our metalsmiths up here? Or do you want to give it a try?"

It was a door of considerable size, with some kind of old-style lock on it. As I reached for the lock, I felt some type of tingling sensation in my hand, and suddenly, the entire doorframe started to sparkle and shoot off sparks. I pulled my hand back quickly, but the flashes continued and spread to the edges of the door. Soon there was a flame that encased the entire door itself. We stepped back and viewed everything that was happening from a short distance. The air filled with an odor that even left a sour taste in our mouths.

Jack said, "Wow, I'm glad that didn't happen when I grabbed it."

As the three of us watched, everything seemed to clear up, including the foul smell and taste finally. All of us looked; the door was still there, and it looked like the fire did nothing to it. I stepped forward and reached out one more time and found no other event taking place. I removed the lock, which was no longer latched as it was a few minutes ago.

Slowly, I opened the door to make as little noise as possible. But suddenly, it squeaked so loud I just flung the door back and looked inside. I walked into the room with Art, Jack, and Steve following in my footsteps, and as we looked around the entire space, we noticed a light coming from one corner of the room. Tom walked in, and all of us made our way in that direction.

What we viewed were the remains of what looked to be a person lying on a bed. As I had seen before with the last dig's remains, I noticed an image standing nearby. However, that vision was very faint.

Steve asked, "Do you see her?"

I said, "Yes, I do."

He replied, "I am sure pleased to hear that as I thought maybe I was losing it, as I can hardly see her."

Jack asked, "See what?"

"We can see a faint vision of a woman standing near the remains," I replied.

As we viewed what was left of her remains, Jack said, "May she rest in peace."

The light we found was some of the fireflies, or whatever the people call them in this region. Someone told us about them when we discussed the homes on the cliffs in Etheral. There was a place for them to live and a jar for them at night to create light. I guess since this room was so dark, they must have thought it to be night most of the time.

Steve asked me, "Do those things have babies and continue to raise little light bugs?"

"I have no idea, Steve, as your guess is as good as what I could come up with, that's for sure," I replied.

There was little more in the room other than a few chairs, pans, and what must have been a sink, a few clothes that could have been towels, and a toilet of sorts. Finally, I said, "I think I have seen enough, and we need to return and let the others know what we have found. Then we need to put those remains to rest."

Chapter 2

What Can You See?

Walking down those stairs, I asked Jack, "Was that a prison or some sort of what we would call a jail cell?"

"I might think it was a holding cell. I hate to think of what it was like to be left there with no help to get out," Jack replied.

Steve said, "To be left, knowing that is where she was going to remain, must have had an effect on her mind."

"I am sure it did, Steve," Jack replied.

Reaching the bottom, we explained what we found. A few wanted to walk up and see the remains and the view we told them about. Our mothers wanted to see the vantage point while the fog was gone. "I would love to see just what is around this location," Catrina said.

Vanessa spoke up and said, "I would like to join you and see that as well."

Soon, a group of people were climbing the stairs and talking about what they might be able to view. Steve, Jack, and I walked around the rooms below to see if there was anything to tell us who that woman was that had been left in that room upstairs left to die a lonely, terrible death.

Walking around and stepping into a few rooms, we each noticed different things of interest, but nothing to inform us as to who was left behind. Jack expressed, "When we can, we need to locate a nice place to bury her."

"I agree, Jack, as it seems her spirit has not been released."

"I guess you and Catrina saw that at that last dig, didn't you?" Jack asked.

"Yes, both of us viewed the spirits that stood near the remains. As I observed this woman, I noticed her as Steve did, standing nearby. However, what we viewed was not like that other situation. What we saw here was only a faint sight of what must have been a woman," I replied.

Steve spoke up and said, "I was wondering if it could be my imagination when I beheld her standing there as it looked almost like somebody was projecting an old photo in the air."

A few of us were standing in front of a large fireplace that had not been used for centuries, I felt Mortice walking up behind us. We heard him speak out, saying, "I think there is more here than meets the eye."

We all turned and viewed Mortice, who had gone upstairs and now returned. Steve said, "I would not be surprised if there were a lot more here than we now see. This entire place looks like a small town site."

Nomi walked up at that time and replied, "I must agree with both of you. What I viewed from above has now led me to believe there are many things here of interest, be it remains, artifacts, or even treasure."

"Treasure would be nice. I mean, to find an old coin or something to keep from here," Steve said.

"I must agree it would be nice to have a keepsake from our time here," I replied.

Everyone was now back down and discussing what they had seen. I spoke out, saying, "We have agreed to place the remains of that woman in the ground to lay her to rest."

Catrina was one of the first to speak up and say, "I think it's one of the reasons we were directed to her."

"You saw her, I gather?" I asked.

"Yes, I viewed a very faint view of what looked to be a woman," she replied.

Steve spoke and said, "So did Marty and I."

I asked all those who walked upstairs, "Did you see her?"

"I am not sure what it was I saw, to be honest with you," was the reply I got from all of them.

Nomi said, "I feel all of us need to get back to the others and clear a path to return."

"It may take some doing with all that overgrowth and brush. It would be nice to find the original path to this town. They must have created a road of some kind to get here. I would even bet that road was made from rock or stone of some kind," John said.

I said, "Let's go back up the stairs and see if we can locate it from up on high."

Bailey said, "The remnants of the woman up there need to be brought down, and I will help anyone who wishes to work with me."

I looked at her and smiled and asked, "Remnants?"

Steve looked at her and then at me and said, "A seldom-used word."

Our mothers, Bailey, and Mortice found a few stout boards wide enough for the remains to lie on and headed back up the stairs.

"Steve, come on, let's see if we can locate a path or road to this place." Both of us ran up the stairs ahead of the others. As Steve and I looked out and around the area below, most of what we viewed had been covered with green. Suddenly, something caught my eye. I asked Steve, "What is that over near that long building?"

He looked, turned his head to get a different view, and then commented, "That could have been a road at one time."

"Exactly what I was thinking," I replied.

Considering our present location and viewing what was below us, we found we had a pretty good idea of where to look. Walking down the stairs, we discussed what we saw with the rest of the people. Steve commented, "We think we have found what used to be a road."

"That would be great if we could use it to enter this place," Nomi spoke out.

Bailey had returned with the others, and everyone placed the remains in a room on the floor. She said, "We will need to bring shovels and allow others to give their final respects."

"Mortice, Nomi, would you two like to join Steve, Tom, Art, and me as we look for that road? Then the rest of the people can follow John back to the wagons and explain what we have found. Who knows? Maybe that road comes out someplace on that path we were using or will be using," I said.

John spoke up and said, "Well, as long as there is still no fog, we should all get moving back to the camp area."

As that group followed him, our little band of explorers walked in a different direction. I sent a thought to Bailey, saying, *You be careful.*

She replied *It seems to me you're the ones that need to be careful because you have no clue as to what is out there.*

"What do you think, Steve? Is it in this direction?" I asked him as I pointed to where I felt we needed to travel.

"I think you're dead on, buddy," he replied.

We had to work our way around a few smaller buildings, lots of brush, and many weird-looking trees with vines in them. We were all amazed at how trees had grown right through the roofs of some of the buildings. We finally approached a long structure after making our way around two or three buildings. We now felt we were near the building we saw from above. It was the long building we had seen, and now it was time to open the doors and see what was inside.

First, we had to use some of our powers to remove a few bushes and trees. Once that was done, we kicked all the rocks and trash out of the way to open the doors.

Nomi and Mortice tried to open the doors and looked back at Steve, Art, Tom, and me, asking, "Okay, I think we need a hand here. Care to help?"

"Sure," Steve remarked.

"You bet," Tom replied.

I said, "Gladly."

Art walked up, saying, "Yes, I probably should help these three as they look pretty weak."

All of us looked at him and chuckled. But he reached up, grabbed a section of the door, and soon the four of us had it moving. It was a long-drawn-out process as these doors had not been opened in centuries.

Both Steve and I used our power to pull the doors open on one side. Tom and Art opened the other side. Looking inside, among all the trees and brush, we found wagons. Some wagons were raised off the ground as if they had become part of a tree, with the tree itself rising through the roof. Some of them were leaning on their sides because of brush and trees that had pushed up alongside them, tipping them over.

Mortice said, "If this was a place for the wagons, I bet if we open those far doors, we will find your road."

Nomi said, "I believe you're correct as it would only seem reasonable that this would enter out onto a roadway."

We made our way through what was left of the building. So much of it had been open to the elements for so long that a considerable amount of what was not stone or rock slabs had rotted away. As we plowed through, moving things out of our way with our powers, we suddenly found out what it means to have a roof falling on us. "Look out!" Mortice yelled as beams and ceiling debris came tumbling down.

I looked up at the same time Steve and Nomi did, reached out with my powers, and said, "I have it." As I moved it to one side, Tom grabbed it and tossed it out of the building. Steve ran over and picked up some of the other debris and gave it a shove, sending it out of the building as well. I looked at him, and he gave me a sideways look, then said, "Well, I just had to keep up with Tom."

Art used his power to remove some of the beams and tossed them out of the way as well. I finished off the rest, and soon it was safe to move on through this area. I would have to say it was an old barn or maybe a storage area for the wagons. As we finished walking to the other end, we did our best not just to toss things aside as we had been doing.

Opening the doors on the other end became a challenge as something was blocking them. Steve exclaimed, "Hey, let's go out this way and clear whatever is in front of those doors." Within a few minutes, all of us scrambled out of an opening in the wall.

Walking around to the front of those doors, we found that a significant amount of rock had rolled out of the side of the mountain and landed right where we didn't need it. All of us put our backs to it and moved all of it out of the way. When we finally had those doors open, we turned and looked around, and what we viewed was a field of green. Trees and brush were everywhere we looked. However, as we viewed the ground, we saw what at one time could have been ground-up rock and slabs of stone moving away from us.

"I think we can follow this and see where it leads," Nomi said.

"I would think you're correct, but I sure hope it's not down the backside of this mountain where we will have to camp out without shelter later this afternoon," Mortice replied.

"Well, we have a pretty good idea of what direction our present camp area is in, don't you think?" Steve asked.

"If we take into account all the turns and travels around the buildings we have recently come past, I think this path or road, whatever it may be, is heading in the direction down lower than our camp," I said.

"Good, let's find out," Mortice said.

I took a moment and thought, *Dad, what is the date back there today?*

Just a moment, son, let me check the calendar. After a few seconds, he replied, *We're still in June. It's the twenty-ninth, Marty. I hope you're doing well. Your mother told me you had all found a small city in the mountains. You be careful.*

We will, Dad, and thank you, and I hope we see all of you again soon.

CHAPTER 3

Beating the Brush

As Bailey and the rest of their group pounded their way back through the trees and brush to return to the other people and our campsite, we headed down a different path.

Catrina asked, "Bailey, do you think those guys will be alright trying to find that road?"

"I am sure they will be just fine unless they run into a huge monster of some kind." As Bailey spoke those words and finished, she started laughing.

"Bailey, can you tell if there are things around us that can harm us?" Wanda asked.

"Only to a small degree, but I have found I can understand the feeling of creatures better lately. It seems I can reach out to a greater distance with my feelings. I keep telling Marty he is the feeling master."

Catrina tipped her head as she looked at Bailey then spoke out and asked, "Are you telling us something about what he feels that your dear mother should know about?"

"Oh, Mom. No, he can just feel animals and any creature days away, and he can tell if they are angry, mad, or have any kind of fear."

"I am sure they will be just fine," Marie told all of them. "Most of us can feel Marty and Steve to some degree out here. If they run into trouble, we will know, I am sure."

"Well, there is the group we left behind, so we know camp is not far off," Bailey said.

"Hey, what did you find up there?" one of the men asked.

"We found a city of gold," John replied.

Suddenly, everyone who had not wanted to walk up those stairs was getting excited about a new adventure. Then John said, "It's not really gold, but it is a small vacant city."

Everyone had questions, and all those who walked up those stairs were trying to answer them as best they could, all the way back to the camp.

"Well, there is the camp," John said.

Walking back to the wagons, everyone wanted to know what all of us had found.

Max said, "There is a small city up there, and the others are searching to see if there is a road we can use to travel on so we can take everyone up there."

Bailey said, "There are remains of a woman that need to be placed in the ground so that she can rest in peace. So when we return, we will need shovels to dig the grave."

One of the women from the excavation crew said, "Mike, you and a few of the other guys grab up some shovels. You may even need a pickax or two."

Someone else said, "We need to clear a path through all that stuff so that we can walk without problems." Suddenly, a group of men gathered up machetes and shovels and headed to the path everyone had just left.

Catrina yelled out, "Hey, let's wait and see what the others find. If they find a better way in there, it would be great, don't you think?"

"Well, that's true, but at the same time, we should clear this way as well," one of the excavation crew said.

Another one spoke out, saying, "It will give us all something to do until they return."

They started to cut and rip small trees out of the ground and slice up brush like it was nothing at all. Some people walked farther out on the path and started to whack away at the underbrush so those following would have an unobstructed route.

Our mothers started to set up for lunch so people would have something to eat after working up an appetite. Vanessa was speaking with Sophia about what they had seen around those buildings. They talked about the construction of each of the structures created by using blocks and slabs of stone. Vanessa was saying, "Those stonework joints looked like they had been cut with a special kind of blade."

Wanda had been listening to the conversation and said, "It sure looked like it. It makes me wonder what kind of saw could have been used back then to slice all that rock from the mountain because they did a great job of creating all of what we observed."

Heather and Krystle were listening to them speaking about the construction, and Heather added, "Not only did they have accurate cuts in everything, but the size of much of that rock and stone had to have taken more than giants to move."

Other people were discussing the fact there might be more small buildings or structures hidden in this forest. Some others were wondering what kind of a hidden city could have been here.

People looking at each other had all kinds of ideas.

While everyone was back at the camp talking about what had been hidden for centuries behind trees, weeds, and lots of brush, our little group continued to walk on a path that would have been wonderful if it did not have trees, fallen rocks, and brush all around and over it. The entire road looked as though it existed of slabs of different sizes cut from the mountain's side. I wondered if this whole city was dug and cut out of the top of this mountain. As we continued to walk, we found ourselves facing a massive opening at the bottom of a rock wall where the road passed through.

It looked like a tunnel of sorts, and it reminded me of some of the ones my parents drove through as we were traveling down the Washington State side of the Columbia River in our world. As my parents would drive along, suddenly, we would enter a tunnel in a mountain section. It was not a long one, but I always loved the thought of passing through them. And of course, my father always had to honk the horn at other cars, and they would honk back.

We were now looking at a tunnel entrance like that last long one we had to travel through a few days ago, back where those two mountains converged, the one we walked and rode through to reach the dig site that had the explosion. That last tunnel going to that camp was not as large as this one. We all looked at one another, and Nomi said, "It looks like they tunneled through the mountain to get in here, so I guess we should see where it goes."

Steve commented, "Maybe it's a good idea to find something we can use for torches. But I guess we will also need something to light those with."

As we entered, we found some brush but few, if any, trees. Nothing like what we had been passing through and around outside. We found torches along the walls, and Nomi pulled out some matches. He lit a couple of them and said, "Steve, you ask, and you receive."

The one thing about this tunnel is it had places like doors along the way, and we forced open one or two to see what they were. I looked up a shaft with a ladder that I surely would not trust. Another opening had small steps cut out of the rock heading upward. Nomi said to me, "I bet that one with the makeshift ladder is an air shaft, as there are openings along the sides up there that would allow the movement of air through this tunnel. Not sure about where those other steps go to."

"This had to take them forever to dig out," Steve said.

"I have to agree, as it seems to go a long distance," Mortice replied.

It looked like the sides had been scraped and sliced straight down on each side as we walked on. The tunnel's roof was just the rock mountain itself as if they had used different kinds of tools to dig through. Mortice and Nomi talked about how far we had come after walking for what seemed to be forever in an enclosed area. Nomi was saying something about this tunnel not being a straight line. Mortice spoke out, saying, "I would guess we have walked about half a mile."

All of us turned and looked behind us to see the entrance, which we could no longer see. As we kept walking, we could tell there was a curve in our route, and soon we were looking ahead of us and viewing a small amount of daylight again.

Shortly, we found ourselves facing a large gate. We noticed a huge metal bar that fell in place to lock it. As the bar fell in place, long rods on each side dropped into place to reinforce it. At least it was on our side. People of height and strength had to handle that as Nomi and Mortice stepped aside, with Mortice saying, "I sure hope one or two of the four of you can remove that because I know we can't."

"Not sure how that locking mechanism works, but we should be able to get that gate open," Steve replied.

I spoke out, saying, "We can sure give it the old college try."

"What kind of try?" Nomi asked.

"Just an old saying from back home about doing what you can to make things happen with education," Steve said.

I managed to move the locking device up, and when it was raised, the bars on the side moved as well. Soon the gate was free to swing open. It squeaked and seemed to groan, and as it did, Mortice said, "It's a good thing you guys were with us, or we would be taking a very long walk back and around to our campsite."

Walking out into the daylight, we started walking away from that tunnel, then turned and looked at the opening and noticed that if someone were to be walking by, they probably would never see it with all the plant growth. Nomi stated, "I am not sure where we are at this moment, but it seems we need to follow those stone slabs ahead of us."

Nomi declared, "One thing for sure, if the forest area existed like this centuries ago, maybe this entrance would not have been very easy to find."

Jack commented, "I certainly have to wonder how long it took just to create that tunnel."

"Looking at the walls and flooring, I would think many years," I replied.

We followed that path for about another twenty minutes. Soon, we ran into another trail of sorts. Nomi said, "I think this is the pathway we have camped on. So, I think we are on the same side of the mountain."

All of us turned around and looked back, noticing the path we came from, was not that easy to see, so we moved some rocks and placed them so we would notice where we would need to turn.

I said, "I feel people in this direction." All of us started walking up the hill on the path heading to where we felt our camp was located. After walking for about another hour, we stopped and Mortice said, "I hear people."

Steve spoke out and said, "I feel our pets and all the other people." Walking farther, we learned we were close to our campsite. All of us looked at one another and shook our heads, and Art said, "I guess that could be a better way to enter that city."

CHAPTER 4

The Entrance

Everyone turned and looked at us as we came up the trail we were planning on traveling down. Bailey walked up to me and said, "I guess you found another way out of that place."

"We did, and we feel it will be a better way to enter that city," I replied.

"Someone needs to yell at those clearing a path to those steps and tell them we may have a better entrance," one of the crew members yelled.

Nomi said, "Let's not get hasty yet, as we may need that entrance as well. So let them continue to clear those steps as they built them for a reason, I'm sure."

Mom spoke out, saying, "Well, at least yell at them to get something to eat. They have been working on that clearing for a good long time. Please tell them we will start serving food soon."

It did not take long for everyone to arrive and get in line for food. As everyone was eating, Steve, Art, Tom, Nomi, Mortice, and I spoke about what we had found, and everyone wanted to walk that path to see what we would face if we wished to return that way.

After eating, it did not take long before people gathered to find out about that tunnel and ask questions.

"How far is it?"

"Do we need any shovels?"

"Can we take a wagon?"

One person asked, "Do we have to walk very long and far?" The questions kept coming, and we answered them as best as we could.

"All of you who can handle the walk and use a shovel, machete, or ax can join us, and those who can't need to remain here and guard the camp," Nomi said.

I could feel lots of excitement as we walked out of our camp and back down the trail. We all turned at the location a few of us walked out from about an hour before. Yes, there were trees and brush just like at the other entrance. We had a few with us clearing some of the thick brush ahead of us and soon heard someone say, "Wow, this looks like a roadway created centuries ago." The crew was excited to see it, as they knew it was a road to a new adventure.

Everyone helped remove the brush and did what they could to clear a path around any trees instead of removing or destroying them. Soon we looked back, and we could hardly see the route we had left and where this roadway ended. But what we viewed was a path our wagons could use. "We are making headway, it seems," I said.

"Headway? I guess that's another one of those off-world words I sometimes hear," Jack said.

"I guess it could be, Jack, as it means we are making progress," I replied.

One of the men up ahead of us yelled out, "I see a large opening in the side of this mountain."

Nomi yelled back, "Good, it's about time. Once we are there, we won't have to work with trees and brush anymore for some time."

We soon took a break from clearing a trail as we walked through the tunnel area. People kept asking about the doors along the way. So we opened a few so they could see what I had seen earlier—metal ladders and small steps.

One of the doors was slightly different, though, and Steve asked, "How come this door is different from those others?"

I replied, "I am not sure, but it is. So, let's take a look and see."

Steve and I walked over as one of the crew brought a shovel our way to help us get a handle on the edge. We wedged the shovel in place and, with our strength, pulled it open. Behind this door were steps, not a metal or a wooden ladder or small rock steps, but what looked like actual stairs cut out of the rock going upward.

I said to Nomi, "This is different from the other places along the way, and I think it deserves a look-see."

"Right, take a few and check it out. The rest of us will continue because we will have to clear more on the path up ahead."

"Let's go, Steve. Bailey, care to join us?"

"Hey, how about Art and me?" Tom asked.

"You bet, let's get it done," Bailey replied.

So the five of us and our pets started the climb.

The steps had been cut out of the rock as a spiral staircase, and as we reached the top, we found an area that was a long hallway. There were shutters on the outside of windows all along this hallway. Max asked, "What is this place?"

Bailey said, "It seems there should be weeds, trees, and lots of brush in this area, but there is little, if any."

I walked over and tried to open one of the windows with the shutters. I finally managed to move the window and pushed the board outside open, but only about a foot.

Looking out, I saw lots of green and a glimpse of what could have been a view of the total area around. "Well, I have a feeling this hallway wraps around most if not the entire city to protect it. I mean, back then, they could have used weapons to take out anyone who would attempt to overtake this mountain."

We walked a short distance down the hallway and found another set of stairs. Steve said, "I have a feeling all these different stairways come up here from different places around the city below."

"I have a feeling you're correct," Bailey replied.

"I can find out where this goes and be right back," Max said.

Within a few minutes, Max returned and said, "That stairway leads into one of the large buildings in town. I can see the entrance to the tunnel on the inside of the mountain, and it's close."

Steve asked, "Do we want to take those stairs and meet the others at that entrance?"

"I guess we can," I replied.

Heading down the stairs, we were soon standing in a large structure made of stone. "There is the entrance to that tunnel," Ziggy said.

As we stepped out of the building onto steps made of more stone, suddenly, we heard all kinds of noise. The brush was crashing around us, and all of us jumped as we watched a few deer skedaddle away from a hiding place.

I said, "I sure did not feel them there, and that was as big a surprise to me as it was to all of you."

CHAPTER 5

Magic Around Us

The others had not arrived yet, so we started walking into the entrance to meet them. "Just a minute," I said.

"What's up, buddy?" Steve asked.

"Do you feel it?" I asked.

Bailey said, "I do feel something, that's for sure, but I am not certain about what it is."

Then Steve said, "Now that you have brought it to my attention, I feel it, but what the heck is it?"

"I'm not sure, but it feels like a very small person. But it seems to be cloaked somehow, as it is hiding from us. We need to find the others and make sure they are safe," I said.

Walking to meet the others, all of us were searching the tunnel walls in every direction. We felt that whatever it could be was getting stronger during the time we walked. Finally, the others came into sight and were shocked to see us ahead of them. Dohadie yelled out, "Hey, what are you doing ahead of us? We left you way behind."

After explaining what we found, the others were interested in seeing the newest find. I said to Mortice, "I think we have company, but whatever or whoever it is seems to be hidden."

He started looking around as others who heard what I said started looking around as well. "I don't see anything, Marty, but I guess that is the whole idea, correct?"

"Come on, let's get everyone out of here, Nomi, so we know these people are safe." People started moving along, and it seemed most of them had no idea about what we felt at all. After every one of us left the tunnel, all of them began to work on clearing the roadway.

Mom asked, "So you felt that as well, correct?"

"Yes, all of us did, including our pets. It's as if someone was camouflaged and watching us. Not sure how they can look like part of the walls in that tunnel," I replied.

"Something sure felt like it was watching us," Steve said.

"I think now that all the others are out of there, I would like to go back in there and find out what it is," I commented.

"Well, if you're going, so am I," Ziggy stated.

Bailey looked at the others in our team and then said, "We're going with you as well."

Tom and Art nodded, and Art said, "We will be at your side."

We walked back inside, and the feeling kept getting stronger with every step. Finally, I felt whoever or whatever it was had to be extremely close. I looked all around, and everyone else with me was doing the same thing. Our mothers were asking each other what they could do to make it appear. Then all of them became silent.

I looked at them, and Catrina sent me a thought, saying, *Look at the wall next to you very carefully, that wall has what looks like small eyes. They were open a moment ago but now are closed, so just keep watching. This is the vision I had a long time ago.*

I moved closer to the wall and studied it more. Suddenly, those eyes opened and scared the living daylights out of me. I jumped and stepped back, then gathered my wits and became composed again. Then I walked up to the wall and reached out my hand, to touch the rocks. All at once, I could feel what seemed to be something brand new. I suddenly got a vision of what a newborn baby would be. I could tell that whatever it was, now was feeling my power. I was now feeling lots of fear and could see a very small section of the wall vibrating, so I moved my hands away from the rock. Soon, what was there started to calm down. I got the feeling it did not understand how any of us could see more than a rock wall.

"I hope you can understand me. Please do not fear us, as we are not here to harm you or anyone else," I stated.

Tom walked up on one side of me, looking at that section of the wall and Art on the other side as our mothers, pets, and the rest of our team gathered close. Everyone was expressing thoughts of interest and amazement.

The eyes we were viewing on the wall were searching in all directions. We watched as the wall began to change, and I could feel it as if it was turning into a new life form. It was turning into what I felt might be a baby or a very small child.

All of us continued to watch what was happening, and I could feel the amazement from all of those around me.

"Do you understand me?" I asked.

I got no reply as we were watching as if a small head was forming and, in the process, was trying to see who or what was around it.

Steve spoke out, saying, "We have seen some pretty weird things since we have been here, but I think this is one of the weirdest I have seen."

Art said, "I have never seen anything like this before on any of the worlds I have visited."

Our mothers were all chatting away. Bailey, Ziggy, Max, and Tabby walked over to me, and Tabby asked, "Uncle Marty, have you ever seen anything like this before?"

"No, I haven't, little one. This is a first for me as well as all of you. I really don't feel whatever this is presents a danger to any of us, however."

Steve said, "Hello there, we are from Earth."

All of us looked over at Steve, including Tom and Art, and started laughing.

Steve said, "Well, maybe whatever this is came from some other planet."

Wanda, Steve's mother, was still laughing as she said, "Son, you may have powers, but sometimes you say things that people just have to laugh at."

All of us nodded our heads and were in total agreement. So I asked whatever it was that we were watching being created, "Can you understand me or even see me?"

She tipped her flowing head to the side and back as if to try to understand what I had just asked. However, I still got no reply.

"I am Marty, and all these people with me are family and friends."

As her body kept forming, even her head now seemed like it was a new bowl of Jell-O. It was shifting and floating as she continued to move her head and look at all of us as I spoke.

Bailey walked over and asked, "Do you understand what we say?"

She seemed to give a very small nod. Then we heard her reply, "Lit bit."

"Well, please join us, and we can learn about each other," Bailey replied.

She pointed at me and then said, "Pow . . ." She stopped speaking for a moment then continued, "Power." She looked like she wanted to say more as her mouth seemed to be forming different words, and finally, she stated, "Power . . . strong."

We continued asking her questions, but it was almost as if she was learning how to speak.

I could feel everyone with questioning thoughts, and I felt maybe they were wondering like me how this thing or person could even talk. But all of us waited and watched.

As she separated from the wall, it was like we were seeing a balloon full of water making the motions. Bailey reached out and tried to grab her, but it was as if she was still somewhat fluid and passed right out of Bailey's grasp. I think all of us were suddenly waiting to see a huge splash of some kind. Our mothers rushed over and helped her to her feet. As she continued to turn into her new life form, Bailey and our mothers tried to comfort and help her adjust. Suddenly, Wanda grabbed a shawl wrap Catrina had around her and wrapped up the new form in front of us.

Wanda turned and looked at all of us and said, "My gosh, you're all staring at a naked person here."

Then, as she tried to walk, she started to fall, and I reached out with my power and caught her. Our mothers and Bailey nearly carried her. They were holding her, helping her to walk, and all the time doing their best to speak with her.

I felt her relax more as they talked to her. Words coming out of her mouth seemed to be all mixed up, but soon we all noticed her form had finally looked as though it was a person and not a mold that seemed as if it was full of Jell-O. She had turned into a very beautiful young woman.

As we walked along, she seemed to have more control of her legs, and her words seemed to be more organized. She said, "I walk."

All of us walked along, and now she was walking, slowly on her own, stumbling now and again. But her hands were there to keep her from falling. As our mothers spoke to her, Catrina asked, "What were you doing in that wall?"

She was slowly trying to explain that she had been floating, it seemed, for some time. As she talked about that, all of us listened closely to what she said. Then as she explained more, that new person tried to put in words how she ended up in the space of the rocks in that wall. Finally, she said, "I become a person again."

Wanda asked, "You became a person again. Were you a person at one time?"

"I . . . live"—and she was trying to breathe and speak and continued with "long . . . time ago."

Our mothers kept asking her questions. She did her very best to answer them. As she was now speaking better, she was trying to explain that it was all of us who set her free in the tower.

As I heard that, I turned and asked, "What is it you just said?"

"I be in tower. Sealed with magic," our newly formed person was saying.

"You were in a tower?" Bailey asked.

"Yes, in tower. Not know how long," she replied.

"How could you have been sealed in any tower and then come to life in the wall of that tunnel?" Art asked.

"Powerful magic. I fear . . . maybe hundreds of years," she continued.

Steve asked, "You were in that tower?"

"Yes, in . . . room," she replied.

"We saw two or three rooms, and one of those rooms had the remains of a person," Steve said.

"Power touched . . . door, spell . . . release me."

I asked, "Are you saying the remains on that bed were you?"

"Door open . . . you walk in . . . bring me . . . back to life," she said.

Bailey and our mothers looked at her, and Bailey asked, "How is that even possible? We saw the remains on the bed ourselves."

Wanda added, "We carried those remains downstairs. So now you're telling us that was you?"

"Long story . . . will . . . tell soon," she replied.

CHAPTER 6

Carter Maye

As we walked out of the mouth of that tunnel, all the girls, Medina, and our mothers were chatting away. I sent a thought to Bailey and asked, *What's her name?*

She turned and looked at me, then changed direction, asking the woman who had just come back to life, "What is your name?"

Bailey sent back a thought saying, *Her name is Carter, Carter Maye.*

We will need to introduce her to everyone after she completes her process of becoming a person again and once all the others get settled.

I agree, she replied.

"I guess our invisible friend is called Carter Maye," I told the guys.

"Interesting name for a girl. I mean Carter, that is," Art said.

Nomi walked up, looked at all of us, viewed Carter, and said, "I see you found a new friend."

"Well, I guess we did," I replied.

Then he asked, "Do you think it's safe to bring the others, all carts, wagons, and coaches in here?"

Tom and I looked all around and then at each other. Steve and Art were doing the same thing, then all of them looked at me. I asked, "What do you guys think?"

"It seems safe enough, and we have enough room for the wagons at this location," Steve said.

Tom commented, "As far as I can tell if we have problems, I feel all of us will handle it."

Art said, "I agree."

Nomi added, "We could get people to start working on that big, long building. Then maybe they can rebuild it so it can be used again to protect the wagons if needed."

"I think that's a good idea, but let me ask a few women if they would feel safe in here," I said. *Mom, can all of you women come over here as we are discussing the idea of bringing the wagons over here?*

She looked over at us guys, spoke to the other women, and replied, *We will be right there.*

As they all walked over to us, they had already been discussing the idea on the way. Catrina asked, "Do any of you feel that bringing all the wagons here would be a problem?"

"Actually, none of us do, but I wanted to make sure all of you had no visions or ideas of things that could harm anyone if we do that," I replied.

"Nomi, if you wish to send a few people back and move the people and wagons in here, we think they would be safe," Medina replied.

Nomi looked over at John and asked, "Would you please get two others and bring the people, wagons, and coaches over here?"

"On my way," he replied.

As all of us walked farther on the path people had been clearing, it looked as though it must go into the center of the town. I asked, "I was told your name is Carter Maye. Is that correct?"

She replied, "My name . . . Carter Maye, yes."

"Do you think there is anything here that is dangerous?" Steve asked.

"I feel all people . . . here . . ." And as she was trying to speak, she was looking all around, then she continued, "Now gone—men who came to kill not here now. So no harm us," she replied.

"Why were you sealed in that tower room?" Tom asked.

"Everyone live here in peace. Outworld not know of us. But we find people talk about city, we see . . . new . . . looks . . . you know, faces. Soon, new faces stealing. New faces hurting others, break what people have. One day, stranger come, tell all a warning . . . some come attack us," she stated.

Tom asked, "A stranger?"

As she continued to speak, it was as if she was learning how to talk better. She replied, "Yes, he talk about people . . . killing giants. They come our way. We have giants . . . we have little people. Ones my size live here. We thought we keep them out. We be very wrong. There is a walk . . . around our town in the high part of mountain."

Steve spoke up and stated, "I believe we found that as it's a walk with windows, correct?"

I added, "Yes. We could hardly get one window to even open, and we had a heck of a time trying to see through all the trees from that walkway."

She said, "Yes. One time, you see forever from windows . . . see people . . . see land below. Walk have areas . . . not all have floor. Sheer cliff . . . no one climb. At least long ago."

It was as if as she became complete; her words and understanding were all coming back.

"Trees grow on cliffs. We see people come up those cliff areas. Trees allow them to climb to city."

"So you had areas that could not be defended?" Tom asked.

"Yes," she replied.

Suddenly, I felt the wagons and people heading our way as I listened. I was still curious about how she had been placed in that tower. I asked, "How is it you ended up in that tower, sealed in that room?"

"When I be young . . . I learn ways of caster." As she mentioned that, she looked at the ground and continued, "I fall in love with wise one. We do everything together. He meet with stranger who warn us."

As I was waiting for the wagons and listening to what Carter was saying, I noticed she was not only looking more like a beautiful woman but even speaking more clearly.

29

Art was interested in that stranger and asked, "Who was that stranger?"

"I . . . not . . . know . . . I never see face," she replied.

"So you and a wise one helped all the people escape?" Jack inquired.

"Yes. My man talk . . . how we save people in city. He tell me of passageway from heart of town. He say underground waterway . . . and . . . steps outside gate."

Art spoke out, asking, "So you got everyone out of the town?"

"He and I got most out . . . lock gates . . . and use magic to hide many who leave. We be cornered with people near us. They have weapons. Our magic was almost gone. We go hide in castle . . . but no way out."

Bailey looked at her as she was starting to cry. Finally, Bailey said, "You know we can talk about this later, if you would like."

She replied, "I think . . . I like that."

All of us felt rather sad at this point because we had a reasonable feeling about what happened to the wise one who was the love of her life. Steve snapped most of us out of it by saying, "I feel wagons and people."

Bailey looked at him and said, "Really, just now? I mean, I was feeling them a long time ago."

I said, "I must agree with Bailey, Steve. When are you going to become a feeling master?"

Tom, Art, Bailey, and Steve all looked at me, then Steve shook his head and started laughing.

CHAPTER 7

Noise and People

Soon all of us stepped back out of the way as the wagons came down the path.

Our mothers and the other girls joined us again. We watched the wagons and people pass by.

As they passed us, those in control of the wagons found a large, cleared area where they could stop or turn around. What I was looking at must have been a large park or something like that at one time. People had cleared out most of it, except the enormous trees, and I was thinking, "They need a good lawn mower now." Men and women were still clearing areas and removing brush. A few were now working on clearing out that long building.

Catrina spoke out, saying, "Before all those other people have the chance to see you, I think we need to get you some clothes to wear rather than just a wrap."

"That be good idea, but my clothes be no more," she replied.

Wanda said, "We can handle that. Follow us." And all of them walked over to the coach that had just arrived.

After finding some jeans, a shirt, and a light jacket, Mom stated, "Now that looks a lot better on you than that wrap."

As she stood there, she stretched, twisted, looked down at the clothes she now had on, then turned and looked at herself in the

31

bathroom mirror, then walked out to the others waiting for her and said, "I like clothes like this. I like this house."

"Well, let's go back out and see what the others wish to do," Catrina commented.

Everyone was excited to see this entire town, a town that had not seen life for many centuries on top of this mountain. I could feel all kinds of excitement from everyone.

Kids were out and about and running here and there, and Nomi yelled at them and their parents and said, "Hey, all of you need to be very careful because we have no idea what is here." So soon, some of the kids came back near the wagons and their parents.

Carter was still speaking with our mothers and seemed to be speaking much better as she told them her home where she used to live was not far away. So all of them talked about taking a walk. As they did, I asked my mother, "How about some company?"

"Are you worried about us, son?" she asked.

"I am, Mom, as I am afraid if you run off too far, things might happen, and you know how much I worry about you."

Our mothers started laughing, and Carter looked at them and asked, "Isn't it a nice thing that your son worries about you?"

All of them shook their heads, and Catrina spoke out, saying, "I think he was giving us back something we gave them earlier. As mothers, we tend to forget they have power and strength. Earlier today, we were all waiting for them to return to camp, and Marty's mother started telling him about how kids should not just wander off."

"Oh, I see, so he was smarking the same things as you smarked out before," she replied.

"Well, I think that is about the general picture of it," she replied.

"Now I see, so that is funny. Yes?" she asked.

I looked over and said, "Yes, that was funny, Carter. Yes."

Bailey asked, "Smarking—could that be equal to the word *doing* or *did*?"

"Possibly," Steve replied.

"How are you feeling?" Bailey asked.

"I am feeling much alive now," Carter replied.

Tom said, "Well, that has to be a good thing, I would think."

Carter asked, "So would all of you like to see where I lived, what must be hundreds of years ago?"

All of us just fell in line and said, "Yes."

Phil asked, "What direction are we going?"

Carter pointed toward what looked like a very overgrown area. So, Phil asked, "How about if we make sure that way is clear before we head in that direction?"

Carter stopped and looked ahead of us and was nodding her head yes, then said, "That might be a good idea because there is much we are not going to get through, it seems."

Phil yelled at one of the soldiers and asked, "Will you please gather up a few others with equipment to clear brush and things and join me?"

"Yes, sir," was the reply.

We all stood there and waited for his men to show up and figured it would be some time before we could advance in that direction. The vines and brush made this entire place look like a jungle.

Mortice walked over and asked Carter, "Where is your water source here?"

"Oh, I will show you as it's a well that is very deep with a stairway to the bottom."

He looked at her and then asked, "Do we have to climb down the mountain to find it?"

"Oh, no, I will show you. We will need some people to cut down brush and growth where we need to go."

Nomi said, "I will send a few of my men with you to help clear some of that growth out for you as you go." So he turned and asked several of his crew to see if they could help clear the way in the direction we had to go. Soon, men and women were chopping down vines, huge bushes, weeds, small tree sprouts, and things like that, leaving large trees standing.

There were a few places we had to wait as they chopped away, but soon Carter said, "Over here," and we looked at a substantial marker on a massive rock of some kind. It looked as though the weather had gotten to it. As all of us walked up, I noticed a carving in the rock that looked like a plaque or honor marker or something.

So I asked her, "Is this a monument for someone?"

"I never knew what that was for. But the man I love showed me this when people come to kill all of us." As she walked up, she placed her hand on part of the wording at the very bottom, and suddenly, something started to move.

She said, "I fear it's stuck because it has not opened in such a long time. It used to move inward so people could enter."

Bailey asked, "Marty, what do you think? Can you open it?"

As I walked up to it, I felt something coming up from the ground, and actually, it was more than just one something, and as I raised my arms, I said in a loud voice, "Everyone, get back."

The opening was only about a foot wide so far, but what looked like bats came swarming out. All of us ducked and dodged them to avoid being hit as they flew out. There must have been about fifty of them that came flying out of that opening.

A few people were now dusting themselves off and looking around to see if they were coming back. Everyone had been shocked, and of course, I was as well, even though I knew something was coming. Walking back to the opening, I felt no more of them rising out of the ground below, so I produced a small amount of power, and at first, I was considering adding more muscle to the push. But slowly, it began to move, and as it seemed to get freed up, it shifted very well.

I looked inside and found a torch and asked, "Who has a light?"

One of the excavation crew walked over and struck a match. Soon I was lighting two more torches from the first one. I handed two of them to the others and stepped inside what looked to be a very large room. I looked around, and there were cobwebs all over the place. I was hoping that the only thing I would find in those webs were tiny spiders that didn't harm a person.

I was looking at those cobwebs thinking of a movie about some spider that placed cobwebs all around a town, and it was big. So far, so good, as I was just brushing them away with the torch. Soon, Tom and Steve entered. Nomi and Mortice followed them. As I have said, this is a large room.

On one side was what looked to be a well. Fifteen feet away, on the other side of the room, was a set of stairs. All of what we were viewing had been cut out of the mountain it seemed. Looking at those stairs, we could see they went down into the depths below. There was an old railing on one side of the steps, but I'm not sure I would trust it after all these years.

Nomi asked, "Have you ever seen stairs like that before?"

"Not exactly like those, but it seems whoever created these made those steps to that walk-around we saw," I replied.

Steve asked, "Walk-around?"

"You know, that place that looks like a hall that we were on, where I tried to open one of those windows," I replied.

He came back with "Oh yes, now I know."

Mortice said, "I bet that rope won't even hold a bucket, but we need to give it a try." Soon he was lowering a bucket down through a hole that was about three feet in diameter.

Nomi spoke out and asked Mortice, "How about I have someone round up a good line to attach to the bucket? I would hate to see it vanish and have to walk, all the way down, to wherever that water is, to find it."

Mortice started pulling the bucket back up and was saying, "Good idea. While you have someone round up the line, I will go back to the wagon and get a water-testing kit."

All of us looked around the inside of this structure while we waited for the line and testing kit. Art said, "They did a great job of creating something that was not real here."

"You mean hiding this entire location or just this area we are standing in?" Tom asked.

"Actually, both if you think about it. What we stand in at this time looks like a massive rock as a recognition monument. However, as we stepped down into this room, we can see people dug out a considerable amount of space here."

"I would not have thought of it as anything else by looking at it from outside. To me, it looked like a huge rock that someone placed words on," I replied.

Suddenly, someone showed up with the line, and Nomi tied it to the bucket. Then, he started to lower it into the well, using both the line and the rope at the same pace. "I hope we have enough line here," Nomi blurted out.

All of us watched and waited as the bucket made its way downward. Some of us walked around and noticed paintings on the walls. I thought it must have been those who built this entire room. It was amazing how they dug this space out and covered it to look like an extremely large rock formation.

We could look up and see the structure of this rock and now understand it was not a rock, but a construction of what looked like cement and rock along with other components to give it the concept of a huge rock. It reminded me of an enormous concrete dome I had seen on TV some years ago.

CHAPTER 8

Locating the Water

Mortice walked in with the water test kit and noticed we already had lowered the bucket, so he set the equipment down, and we just talked about the placement of his guards. He asked, "Do you feel we need to place guards on high ground around here to make sure no one else comes in?"

I thought for a moment, as I had a feeling similar to what I had back when Steve killed that beast, but it just seemed so faint. Other than that, I felt nothing around us that would be a danger. I felt the deer that were still roaming and a few other animals just now settling in, but other than that, nothing. So I replied, "I don't feel any danger around us, Mortice. You may wish to place a couple of the guards near that opening to the mountain we just came out of, but I think we are fine."

Tom said, "I truly find it amazing you can feel people and animals and tell if they are dangerous or not."

"Yes, I could tell when you arrived and how far away you were and knew how much you even traveled."

"No way," he replied.

"Yes way," Steve said.

Mortice said, "I have learned to pay attention to what he says about his feelings because they are on point."

Nomi spoke out, saying, "I have a strong faith in what Marty says when it comes to things that are angry, mad, or hungry and dangerous because he has warned us a number of times."

Art commented, "It seems much of your powers are growing as I can somewhat feel they have increased since we arrived."

"I'm not sure about that. All I know is I feel things and seem to understand those feelings more every day."

"Well, that must be the water, and I think we need to measure this line as we bring it out. That way, we can see how far down we just lowered the bucket."

The bucket was weighted just enough to make it sink in the water, and now it was being raised, with two of the soldiers measuring the line as it returned.

Water splashed over the edges of the bucket as it was pulled over the lip of the well. One of the guards was shaking his head and said, "We only measured one hundred and twenty feet."

Mortice said, "Surely there has to be a mistake because this city sits well over that since the mountain itself must be over three hundred feet from the bottom."

Carter was standing there and commented, "I was told at one time, water for all the buildings came from a pipe in the ground. It rose feely, but I heard some say there is a shutoff of some kind on that pipe where the water comes from. I always thought it was the big valve in the building next to us because they would open the shutoff a little, and as they did, all buildings received water."

Steve asked me, "Could this have artesian water flow?"

"Artesian what?" asked Mortice.

Everyone was waiting for the answer to Mortice's question because they had not heard that word before.

Steve said, "From what I understand, all water flows in layers in the earth, and sometimes you can find places where the water breaks loose from a layer and heads to the surface, and they say it's an artesian water flow."

I sent a thought to Steve: *Did you just make that up?*

Well, it was the best I could do on the spur of the moment, he replied.

"I don't know if this is an artesian or not, Steve, but I guess the only way we can find out more is to go down there and see what's going on," I replied.

A few of us walked over to the steps leading down. I looked over the edge to find out how far we could see and noticed the steps seemed to be created along a wall and open space on the other side. As I started to step down, I felt the levels were extremely solid, so I stepped, one foot after the other, and stayed close to the wall. Soon I must have cleared about a hundred steps. The light from my torch showed me an enormous cavern, and I could hear the water close by.

Tom was right behind me and said, "Look over at that far wall."

As I did, I noticed what looked to be some piping running down to the water. "I wonder if that goes to where that shutoff is located that Carter said was in some building up there."

"Maybe, but we won't know until we find out more about this water that seems to be close by," Tom replied.

Steve and Art had been following Tom and me. Finally, Steve said, "Art, you and I should see if we can find that shutoff Carter was talking about, as it looks like that pipe is heading up and over to the right up there."

"Well, let's see if we can find it while they locate that water," he replied.

We continued down as Steve and Art headed back up. Reaching the top, Steve asked Carter, "Do you know where we can find that water shutoff?"

She said, "I believe I do, but not sure. Come with me, and let's see if I am correct."

A few people followed them to a building that was not far away. But they were having difficulty just walking to it. There were vines and brush, along with trees that had grown over the many years, basically blocking their way. Nomi called a few other men over and asked them to bring machetes. Soon, about six men showed up and were chopping away.

Once a path was cleared, the next problem was getting into that building. First, a tree had grown up right in front of the door. So it looked like a window that had been broken out was the next step in the process. As a few climbed through the window area, Steve followed them and was soon standing in a room with pipes that looked to be made of a concrete and metal mixture. At any rate, vines, brush, and cobwebs had to be cleared away just to see what was there.

Carter was standing outside the window and said, "I think over there in that section is a shutoff and turn-on of some kind. I am not sure if it will even work after all these years." Soon the men that had entered the building were chopping away at vines and different kinds of brush.

Suddenly, a noise was heard, and Steve turned just in time to see a snake moving toward him. He yelled, "Snake!" Then he looked for a place that would be high ground. He found what he was looking for, climbed up, and looked down at the snake slithering around below him.

One of the excavation crew asked him, "Aren't you the one that killed that Metathesis?"

He looked down at the man with an awkward look on his face and very slowly said, "Yes, that was me, but I hate snakes."

"Well, you killed a creature that was part snake and about fifty times the size of this little guy. Why didn't you just blow it away?"

Steve looked at him and said, "I guess I let my fear overload my brain."

The man who commented about the snake took his shovel and ended the snake.

"Over here!" one of the men yelled, and soon all of them walked over to what looked like an old, rusty, mold-covered handle. "We need something to clean this with and some rags." one of the men said.

One of the people outside said, "Here is some old material. See if this will work."

After cleaning the handle and trying to turn it, they found it was solidly in place. Steve said, "Well, we have an idea where the shutoff is, so now we need to get a few people over here to clean this room out and work on that fitting."

"Here is another door. Let's go out this way," someone said, and soon people were pushing and shoving and not making any headway.

Steve looked back at the window and saw Carter and asked her, "Could you please go to the backside of this building and let me know what is there keeping this door closed?"

"Just give me a few minutes," she replied. She turned and asked some of those standing near her outside, "Can you help me clear away to the back of this building?" Soon they had cut their way around the back and found there were a few good-sized rocks by the door that had fallen away from a building close by.

"Steve, big rocks are holding the door in place," one of the men yelled.

"If I give enough of a push and they move, will they damage anything?"

"I don't think so," Carter replied.

"Please get away from that door and make sure no one else is near it," Steve said.

All of them ran back around the corner of the building. Then one of the men yelled, "Go for it, we are around the side of the building now."

Steve let it rip just enough to see the door move, and then he placed his hands around his mouth and blew just a bit more toward the bottom of the door. Soon the doorway was clear, including the door itself. "Let's go see if they found anything interesting down below," Steve said.

Some men stayed to clear the room out, with one man leaving to round up some oil to treat the valve to free it up. Steve was now standing outside with the rest, and Carter asked, "How did you do that?"

"Well, it's a long story," Steve replied.

As everyone gathered to find out what both groups learned, Steve said, "I think we found the control for the water for these buildings.

However, it's going to take some effort to get that valve freed up and working again."

"We found the same kind of problem down below. The entire section we climbed into was a vast cavern, and what we found for water was a pipe stuck into the ground. It has a very small pipe attached to it with a flow of water running out of it that fills up a large hole in the ground. When we dropped that bucket for water, it landed inside that hole. Over the years, the water just filled that dug-out cavity and ran out into a large path through the rocks and drained off," I stated.

"So is the water coming up in that pipe an artesian flow?" Nomi asked.

Tom replied, "We think it is, and that's why they were able to harness the flow down below and create a well. That water slowly flowing below was set up before running the pipe up to whatever room you found. It has a valve down there just above the small pipe protruding from the large pipe that drips that water into that hole."

I added, "It seems whoever found that water source managed to place a pipe in the hole as the water continued flowing. It looks like they used cement or some kind of sealant around that pipe base to make sure it would remain in place."

Tom continued, "The idea they used was a sound one because that valve must have been open until all the cement, or whatever they used, hardened. When they shut off the valve, the water stopped flowing. After they managed to cap off the water down below, they started adding more pipe to that one section above the valve."

"Mortice said the water is good to drink. So, we now have a good source of water here," Bailey commented.

CHAPTER 9

Finds and Food

"Well, I guess now we need to make sure and find locations for the townspeople to sleep other than that old wagon and on the ground. I mean, it seems there are plenty of places for them to clean up and sleep in," Wanda said.

Everyone gathered near the wagons. Our mothers and Medina were speaking about learning more regarding the lives of those who lived here. "Carter, we need to learn more about all the people that lived here," Catrina said.

"Not sure what you wish to know, but I will tell you what I can," she replied.

After a few hours, everyone was sitting and asking questions and getting answers. We learned that most of these people were here when the wise ones came over to help the giants. The people attacking this small city were also a few of the ones that were killing the giants and stealing from them.

Nomi walked over and told us, "That long building is almost cleaned out. If anyone wants to put their wagon in there for more protection since the fog seems to be setting back in, we can move them now."

Carter said, "Most of the time, we had no need for fires burning as there was no fog. It was normally warm around here, so the fog stayed away. So I remember times we didn't burn fires."

"No fog?" Jack questioned.

"We live on a mountain that is lower than others around us, and this one never had fog until we started getting people we did not know showing up, stealing, and hurting others. The man I was in love with, being a wise one, did something and then we started to have fog that would hide our city," Carter stated.

Jack looked at her and tipped his head a bit to the side and asked, "Did he cast a spell of some kind that created a fog?"

"I do not know for sure," Carter said.

"Well, let's set up campfires around different areas and see if that gets rid of it," Steve said.

"I will give you a hand, Steve," Art commented.

"I will too," I added.

Soon, I heard Tom say, "A good old campfire is always a nice thing to see. So I am with all of you."

As we walked around and gathered up wood, we set up different locations around a large area that looked like a good amount of space where heat could collect. I sent a thought to my mother and asked, *Please see if one of the guards can walk around and light these piles on fire for us? We don't have any matches.*

I will ask Phil, as he is close.

Thank you, Mom.

Soon, Phil was walking around, lighting the bonfires. With the fog setting in again, it took some time for the warmth to affect it. Many of the people were clearing areas around those fires to make sure they didn't spread. Many of the children gathered more wood and stacked that in piles near each of the bonfires.

Others were moving a few of the wagons into the large, long building. We found some of those wagons that were in there still seemed to be in fair condition and could be used. Tom declared, "That is amazing. I wonder how long they have sat here or been tipped over and are still in workable condition?"

Dohadie said, "It looks like we have more wagons now."

Burdock said, "Only one problem, brother, we don't have any other horses to pull them."

All of us guys laughed. Steve said, "You know, Dohadie, he got you on that one."

"Yes, he did, as I was not thinking about that."

We moved some of the old wagons around and placed them on one side of the building as our other coaches were being brought in and set up. Everyone was walking around and checking things out in the large building. There were tools and items the excavation crew found to be exciting finds. "Look at this," one was saying to another. Others were speaking out, commenting, "Look at how perfect this is."

There were so many great new finds from many centuries ago in this one location. People could not stop looking at everything. Some of the people came walking over to us, with one of the women saying, "We think we have found an excellent place to cook. So if we have a few that wish to help all of us clean it up, we may have a great place to prepare meals. But we can't get started until that entire location is cleaned."

Manna Day said, "I am with you, so let's get started."

Wanda commented, "Let's get to cleaning."

A good number of men, Vanessa, and our other mothers joined in, and Vanessa asked, "What? A real kitchen?" Soon all of them and some others walked off to find out what needed to be cleaned.

One of Nomi's crew walked up, stating, "The kids have found a good location for target practice, and I am sure pleased all those kids are on our side."

"Well, we have to agree with you on that," Steve replied.

Soon a few of the townspeople were sitting around one or two bonfires and laughing and enjoying the evening like it was just a fantastic campout. Many of us walked back to the first building we walked into, and Tom asked, "Didn't Carter say the love of her life saved her by sealing her in that room as others were climbing the stairs to kill them?"

"I think that is what she was saying, and I got feelings from most around us, as she said that he did not live," I replied.

"I got that feeling too," Steve added.

"So, what happened to him if he saved everyone in the town and made sure the woman he loved was safe?" Art asked.

"Maybe they captured him and dragged him off, then killed him too," Tom replied.

"I guess that's the question, isn't it?" I asked.

Art, Tom, Steve, and I walked back to the room where everyone had placed Carter's remains, and as we looked around, all we viewed were the boards they had put them on.

I asked, "If two people had killers chasing them and they ended up climbing those stairs, and he sealed her in that room to protect her, wouldn't his remains be around here someplace?"

Steve said, "Let's walk upstairs and look around more than we did before."

"There is the room she was in, and these two other rooms are empty. There are not a lot of other places a person could have been hiding up here, that's for sure," Tom said.

As I was looking at the openings around this hall and space, I started to think maybe he climbed out of one of those. So I said, "There is one other thought, and that is we should look outside of these openings they used to see all around."

All of us walked over to an opening about three feet tall and around a foot and a half wide and open to the air. Each of us picked one and looked outside. All I viewed were trees and lots of them. Tom was looking out one of the others and turned around, walked back toward me, and said, "If he went out that opening, he must have flown away."

Art said, "Nothing over here except a thirty-foot drop. If he had jumped from here, he would have landed on all kinds of rocks. But of course, those might not have been there at that time."

Steve said, "Take a look at this."

All of us walked over to that opening and looked out one at a time. What we viewed was a large rock slab covered with dirt over the years. The center of that rock slab looked like a large pile of dirt. Covered with brush and branches, however, it was about the width and length of what a person could be. Maybe it was the person that helped all those people and saved Carter. However, from where we stood, it only looked like a lot of dirt and such, with branches and brush covering it all.

"What do you think, Tom?" I asked.

Tom replied, "That could possibly be his remains covered with centuries of dust, dirt, and debris."

"I think we need to go down there and see what's there. If it is a person, we will need a way to recognize him if that's his remains," Steve remarked.

We walked back downstairs and managed to make our way near the building on the outside but not close enough to even see if it was him. I sent a thought to Vanessa: *Vanessa, do you see Nomi any place around you?*

He's standing right here, Marty. What do you need?

Can you please ask him to bring a few of his men over to where I am waving my arms around to help us chop down a lot of brush? I asked.

Just a sec, she replied.

I noticed her looking all around, and I started jumping up and down, waving my arms, then Steve, Art, and Tom did the same thing. She finally turned in our direction, noticed us, and started laughing. Then I saw her speaking to Nomi, pointing in our direction.

She said, *Nomi is on his way.*

Thank you, I replied.

Soon, Nomi and a few of his men were walking up to us with several different tools. They began cutting down all the brush between us and the wall and what we thought might be the remains that lay next to it.

After about an hour of us working up a sweat, we were looking at an area that had been cleared. Finally, we were able to stand near what was a dust- and dirt-covered large rock slab. In the center was what looked like a small mountain range, sheltered with branches and debris, looking natural as if it was just part of the surroundings. Nomi asked one of his men to run over and locate a small broom and a few brushes.

I could feel the anticipation in all of those around me as we looked at what we hoped would be our answer. Soon a man arrived with several smaller brushes and a broom. He handed brushes to all of us, and then he stepped up on the slab of rock and started sweeping the dirt around the section in the center. Nomi asked another man, "Please run and grab a screen so we can make sure to sift this dirt."

One of his men left and returned and, with the help of two others, set up the screen over a large tarp. They started to gather all the loose dirt that was swept into a pile. He told us, "We need to sift all that dirt to be sure nothing else is there." We waited for them to remove that separate pile of dirt.

There were now locations around the mound where everything had been swept away. Then we started to brush off the dirt from the top of that small mountain range. Slowly, we made sure not to damage anything if it was a person. As we brushed, we were hopeful on the one hand that we would find the love of Carter's life but, on the other hand, hoping this was just a pile of dirt.

As we removed the dirt and debris, it became evident this was the remains of a person. The men screening the soil suddenly stopped, and Nomi asked, "What is it?"

"Not really sure," was the reply from one of his crew.

All of us turned and looked at what might have been a ribbon or something like that.

"Please set it aside and keep looking," Nomi said.

We now knew it was a person and could have been someone who jumped from an opening up above. We were lucky to even find him after all these years, and I guess it's because he landed on a large rock slab. A slight overhang around the top of this tower might have kept most of the weather off him. Nothing had grown up through the slab but had grown all around it. The crew was still trying to remove some of the remaining brush so others could get closer.

Art asked, "Do you think it's a good idea to have her look at this?"

Steve spoke up, saying, "It might be a lot for her to handle at this time."

Tom and I both agreed. I said, "I think what we need to do is discuss with her more about what happened. Then maybe we can bring her over here later, to see if there is a way she can identify him."

They agreed, and Tom replied, "I feel that would probably be better than just dragging her over here and saying, 'Look.'"

We asked Nomi if he could find a tarp now that the remains were in the open. So he sent one of the men over to bring something over and place it over the bones without damaging them.

All of us looked around to find the rest of our crew, mothers, and Medina. We were hoping to find Carter with them, but at this time, I didn't see her. As we walked up to all of them, I asked, "Is Carter around?"

Mom said, "She found her old home and wanted to see if there was anything thing left from her family or the man she lost."

"We may have found the man she lost," I said.

"What did you say?" she asked.

I said, "I think we found his remains."

"Don't you think we should tell her?" she asked.

"I think we need more information," I replied.

Many of them had been grabbing a bite to eat, so I said, "I am hungry."

Mom asked, "Marty, don't you feel she needs to know? The sooner the better?"

"We discussed this before coming over here, and all of us feel it would be better if we talk with her and make sure she will be able to handle that impact," I replied.

CHAPTER 10

Feelings of Loss

As most of us were sitting around eating, some of the other people showed up that had been out exploring the area. They looked like they were as hungry as the rest of us. It was just after those people arrived that one of the men from the excavation crew came in and said, "We just managed to take care of our food for a good day or two."

I was thinking about those deer we had seen earlier as he said that and asked, "Not one of the deer we saw earlier, was it?"

"Oh no, we were thrashing around through the brush and almost got gored by a Dorga," he replied.

Bailey asked, "What is that?"

Vanessa said, "It's like Agatha as a pet, only bigger, meaner, and more dangerous with a very long snout and big horns coming out of its mouth."

Steve spoke up, saying, "That sounds like a wild boar."

"Well, it's out here if you wish to see it," he replied.

Many people walked out to see what they had brought us for dinner for a few days. There it was, just as Steve mentioned. "Yup, that looks a lot like what I have seen in photos of a boar," Steve said.

All of us looked at it, and Nomi asked John, "Would you please grab one or two of these brave hunters and haul that thing off and prepare it?"

"Come on, guys. You killed it, and now you get to skin it and dress it out," John said.

Carter walked up, and I asked her, "I hear you found your home and were looking for memories. Did you find anything?"

"I found a few things. I had to chop down lots of weeds, brush, and even had to move around a tree growing in what used to be my living room, but it was still my home," she replied.

"What was his name, Carter?" I asked.

"What was whose name?" she asked.

"I guess he was your boyfriend. The love of your life who saved you," I stated.

"His name was Zane, Zane Davain," she replied.

"Do you have any idea what happened to him?" Steve asked.

"No. Not really. All I remember is Zane opened the door, told me to lie down and go to sleep. And that is all I remember. I must have fallen asleep as soon as I lay down," she stated.

Jack walked up and heard that and asked, "If I recall, you stated he was a wise one. Is that correct?"

"Yes, he was. He and I saved most of the people that lived here, as we fought those who invaded our city. He was powerful compared to me. We opened the door to the cavern, and he rushed people down the stairs. While he did that, I guided people to the upper gate, watched them running down the steps, and locked that gate. I returned and we got most of the people out before other people came over the walls."

"What did he look like?" Tom asked.

"He was taller than me, but he was in pretty good shape for his size. I remember how he used to pick me up and swing me around. We were so much in love." All of us saw tears as she was speaking, and Bailey asked her, "Did you get something to eat?"

She took a deep breath, shook her head a bit, and then I felt her relaxing after Bailey asked that question. Then she replied, "No, as a matter of fact, I am starving as I have not eaten for hundreds of years." Then, all at once, all of us started laughing, and I felt she was doing much better now.

"Come on," Bailey said.

As we walked over to the building where others were already eating, she stopped, turned, and looked at the tower. She stood there for a few minutes with all of us just standing there looking at her. Then unexpectedly, she said, "You know it's as if he's still here, and I can feel his being near."

All of us looked at each other, with looks that showed all of us were stunned.

Jack asked, "Is that just because you see that tower, or is it an actual feeling of him?"

She turned and looked at Jack, and the look on her face was one that showed us she seemed to be feeling something. As she turned to speak to Jack, I could feel what she felt. As I was looking at her, I had the feeling he was here, and as I got that feeling, I turned and looked over to where we found those remains.

She replied to Jack, saying, "It's an actual feeling of him being near me." Then she turned and started walking over to the area we had cleared. All of us looked at each other amazed.

I walked ahead of her and stopped her, then asked, "Hey, I thought you had a few hundred years of hunger?"

She seemed to snap out of it and looked at me, saying, "You are correct. I am starving." Then all of us headed to the area with food.

"Tom, she felt him and was actually going to walk right over to those remains if I had not stopped her."

"Why did you stop her?"

"I can feel a lot of her feelings, and right now, I think if she sees those remains without eating and all of us talking to her, she might freak out on us."

"But she felt him?" he asked.

"Yes. She did feel him, and I could feel him as well."

"Is he actually there? I mean, like she was and came back?" Jack questioned.

"No, I don't get that impression, but there is a strong attachment between him and her even today," I replied.

All of us talked about the city and the cavern. After getting something to eat, many people went back to work, with some walking down those steps to the location where that pipe had been placed in the ground. And others were now working on that valve in the building above.

Our mothers and all the girls were talking with Carter. They were learning more about Zane as she was eating. I had the feeling she was still getting waves of his being around here still. As she started talking more without crying, I felt maybe we were getting close to finding out if she knew of any way to recognize his remains.

She was saying, "When we first ran into each other, he just stopped, and so did I. We both stood there looking at each other for the longest time, then he said to me, 'You and I are already in love.'"

"Really?" Wanda asked.

"Yes. I felt that as well," she replied.

Catrina asked her, "What if we do find him? How will you know it's him?"

She looked directly at Catrina and replied, "I will know as we had a love so strong that even today if we only find his bones, I will know if it's him."

All our mothers had discussed what we had already found before Carter came back. Wanda asked Marie, "A moment, please," and she moved her head to the right as if to give her a direction. Once the two of them had some distance between Catrina and Carter, Wanda asked, "Did Catrina just let the cat out of the bag?" Both women looked at each other.

I was standing near the two of them and said, "I feel she hasn't because Carter is more formidable now that she had something to eat. She seems to be mentally and physically stronger, and I don't think she took what Catrina said as a situation that has taken place."

I sent a thought to Catrina asking, *Have you seen something lately?*

I have. I saw Carter with a man, holding him and kissing him, she replied.

What? Dead? I asked.

No, very much alive, with all of us around them. I think all of us need to go for a walk near what you found.

It's just bones.

Somehow, and I am not sure in what way, he is going to live again, Catrina stated.

I have the feeling anything is possible, let's all go for a walk, I replied.

"Carter, why don't you join us as all of us go for a walk?" I asked.

"Sure, that would be great as there is so much here to see," she replied.

All of us looked at one another and stood up, and I took the lead and walked past the area we had found. As soon as we walked by those bones, Carter stopped, and I felt it. I turned and looked at her and asked, "What is it?"

The bones were probably a good fifty feet away with lots of brush, trees, and rubble between us and all around that slab, but she was feeling him. I was feeling him. She started making her way over to that large rock slab. When she got there, she kneeled and started crying. Medina walked up and placed her arm on Carter's shoulder and was talking with her. I could feel very little difference in her feelings, but there was a calm coming over her, and Medina sent me a thought saying, *I can't stop all her feelings of loss, but I may be able to make her feel calmer.*

I can feel that happening right now.

Good. I think she will find peace and comfort in knowing we found his remains. She still needs to be sure this is him. We need to see if she can recognize anything here, Medina said.

All of us stood there feeling lost in the feelings of Carter crying. I personally sensed all of what she was feeling. Steve walked over to me and said, "I feel what she is feeling."

"That's good. I feel it too."

Bailey walked up and asked, "What was that all about?"

"Do you feel what she feels?" I asked.

"Yes, I do," she replied.

"Steve was just telling me he felt what she was feeling as well."

Bailey walked up to Carter and Medina, then kneeled next to them. Carter reached out and placed her hand on the bones of his hand and said, "This is his ring." Then she really started to cry.

Bailey asked, "Are you sure this is Zane?"

Carter replied, "Yes, this is his ring, and I can feel him. I can really feel him."

Bailey, is that really him? I asked.

Yes, and you must feel what I feel right now as well, she answered.

I do. It's a strong feeling of a connection that I don't understand, but maybe I can do something about that, I replied.

What can you do? He's long gone, Marty, she replied.

I stepped back away from everyone and thought, *Anubis, can you hear me? Anubis, can you hear me?*

What seemed to be forever was probably only about ten minutes. So I tried to reach him again.

Anubis, my friend, if you can hear me, I need your help.

I can hear you, but who is this? Who is it that would disturb the god of the dead?

Anubis, it's me, Marty.

Is this my buddy?

Yes, this is your buddy.

I knew that. I just wanted to hear your reaction. Then I heard him laughing.

I see you have not forgotten.

No, I have not forgotten at all, my friend. How are you doing?

We have had a lot of events happening, but I have a question for you.

What is it?

If someone has been dead for hundreds of years, is it possible to bring them back?

It depends on the life of that person.

What do you mean?

If he or she was honorable, it might be possible. However, if that person was a thief or liar and dishonest, I would have to say it would be tough to do.

Can you figure out where I am now?

I know exactly where you are now, he replied.

A wise one saved many lives in this city and sealed the woman he loved in a room to keep her safe. Unfortunately, it looks like he tried to escape the killers but jumped to his death, landing in front of me.

I understand, Anubis replied.

I believe he was a wise one who protected and saved many lives here.

I know where you are, and I feel there are people near those bones. Can you ask them to move?

Right now?

Yes, please ask all of them to move way back.

Please give me a few minutes to move them. One of those women is the one he sealed in a room in that tower. I brought her back to life after hundreds of years when I broke the seal on the place she was in.

Marty, it sounds like you should be the protector of the dead.

No thanks, I replied.

I walked up to where Bailey, Carter, and Medina were kneeling. I said, "I need all of you to move back at this time, way back away from this place." I sent a thought to Medina and Bailey: *I have an idea of how to bring him back, and I need all three of you to move back with the rest of the people here.*

Soon, Bailey and Medina stood up, but Carter was crying and said, "Please leave me with him."

I walked over to her and said, "I need you to move right now as I am going to see if we can bring him back to life."

She looked at me and replied, "You must be a powerful wise one."

"I am no wise one, but I have an idea that may work," I stated.

Bailey came back and helped Carter to stand. She was crying but doing as I had asked.

I turned to everyone around us and said, "I need all of you to stand farther back."

I think there is room now, Anubis, I said.

Unexpectedly, the ground started to shake. Dust and dirt were blown into the air. Brush and trees were moving and being tossed from the ground. It was as if the earth was opening and out of the land rose what looked like a very ugly dog, in very fancy-dress garb. It was Anubis.

Everyone around me was starting to get in defense mode. I noticed how everyone stepped back, and I got the feeling from Tom and Art that they were surprised and ready to fight. Of course, even our pets were there and about to raise weapons. I yelled, "Stop where you are. This is my friend."

Art and Tom looked at each other, then back at me with their mouths open and comments that did not come. Finally, as Art was looking at me, he raised his hand, palm up, and pointed at Anubis, then commented, "I know who he is."

I said again, "This is a friend, so please do nothing. Just step back and let us see if we can do the impossible."

As Anubis arrived, he stood there in a stance of authority with his staff in one hand and dressed in clothing that seemed to be designed for a person of status. He looked around at everyone and everything here. If I had not walked up to Anubis, I am sure I would have seen a large hammer coming into view by Tom with a charge of lightning reaching the sky. I had the feeling Art now knew something of what I had in mind. As I walked up, I felt the two of them back off a bit and slowly watch what was taking place.

Art was standing next to Tom, telling him who Anubis was. "I have heard of him over all the years I studied many old civilizations," he was saying.

People had been running and hiding, jumping and yelling as the dust flew when Anubis appeared. That began to stop as I walked forward to see an old friend. As he arrived, he was his tall self, so I grew in height alongside him. I had forgotten how it felt to grow in size. However, now Anubis and I were looking into each other's eyes. Everyone was in total awe as I was now the same height as him. I reached out my arm, and he did the same. We grabbed each other's forearms with our hands in a greeting of genuine friendship.

As Anubis and I spoke, he viewed all of those around us, then looked down at the bones on the large rock slab below. "I remember this one, from many centuries ago, as I felt he was not ready to be removed. I feel he was a man of honor and had saved many lives, and I could also feel he was truly in love." As he said that, he turned and looked directly at Carter, pointed at her, and continued to say, "With that woman."

"I understand that to be true," I replied.

"You told me he saved her. Is that correct?"

"The remains you see below us are those of a being who could create great magic, and he placed her in that tower above us, keeping her safe and protected as he placed a spell on her room. My power removed that protection when I touched the door, opened it, and entered that room—the room where she had rested for hundreds of years."

"So, my friend, what is it you ask of me?" Anubis asked.

"I hope you have a way to restore his life," I replied.

He said, "My friend, I owe you much. I am not sure I can do what you ask, but I am going to do all I can to make it happen."

"Thank you, my friend."

He turned and looked at Carter and said, "I must take these bones with me if I am to try to return him to your arms."

She looked at him with tears in her eyes, almost crying, and asked, "Can you please bring back the one person I love more than life itself."

"I will do what I can, child," he replied. With that, a mist appeared, and both Anubis and the remains were soon gone.

Carter started crying more. I became my regular height again, then walked over and placed my arms around her, and said, "Anubis is the protector and guide for the dead. If anyone can help us at this time, I feel it is him, and that is why I contacted him."

She moved back away from me a bit and looked at me with a questioning look, then asked, "You contacted that being we just viewed from the dead?"

"Yes, he is a friend."

Tom said, "Marty, you're full of surprises."

Steve commented, "He needed our help, and we gave it to him."

Bailey said, "We helped him get his power back along with that staff."

"That sounds like a tall tale I might like to hear," Tom said.

Art said, "I think I would love to sit in that learning session."

Max, who had been standing near us all that time, spoke out and said, "Don't forget I took him flying with me."

"You did what?" Tom asked.

Art asked, "Can you fly, along with changing?"

I said, "Max is a wonder of all wonders as he can change into almost anything."

Steve, Bailey, I, and the rest of our pets all nodded, with Tabby saying, "I loved how Max turned into a huge bird and flew away with him."

Tom and Art were now looking at all of us, just shaking their heads.

Art commented, "Yes indeed, that is a learning session I will not miss."

CHAPTER 11

Getting Answers

Everyone was standing there asking questions and talking about what they had just watched. Finally, Tom asked, "Bailey just said you helped him get his power. How did you achieve that?"

"He was being held in a camp, just like many others in slave labor. Anubis had no choice but to guard them. Someone managed to take his staff. That staff is a great source of his power, and all of us worked to help him find and get it back, which in turn set him free and helped us free all of those at that camp."

Art asked, "How did you manage to gain such height?"

"It's just one of those things we can do," I replied.

"Who are 'we'?" Art asked.

"Steve, Bailey, and me," I said.

Our mothers and Medina walked Carter over to a large area where they could sit and talk without others bothering her. Carter asked my mother, "How could he bring the dead here to help me bring Zane back?"

My mother said, "Carter, I don't know all the things he can do. He has powers that most of us can't even understand. He can do things none of us can do. Steve, Bailey, and Vanessa seem to have many of the same kinds of powers and strengths, but they are not as advanced as Marty's."

"He took his bones and his ring, and that's all I had left of him. What if he can't bring him back?" she asked as she was crying.

"We need to wait and see what will happen. If Marty didn't think he could help, he never would have reached out to him," Catrina stated.

Over the next few days, all our pets had been following Masher around the city in places most of us could not even get to. They had been searching and making sure nothing was here that could harm all of us.

During all that time, Carter worried and wondered if she would ever see his bones again. She spent lots of time with Bailey and our mothers as she asked Medina many questions about bringing people back.

Medina was saying, "I am not sure what is going to happen. So many gods do things that ordinary people cannot even think of. For example, Anubis is one of the early gods who has always protected the dead. He was also known as being a person who showed others how to prepare, clothe, and treat the dead as they would enter their final rest."

"Marty, can you please join me?" Mortice asked.

I turned and replied, "Sure." Then I walked over to where he was standing.

He and a few of the guards looked at different places and found the remains of people and animals. He pointed to something that looked like a creature Steve had killed sometime back that had attacked Bailey and our pets. I noticed that it didn't look like it had died all that long ago. I walked up closer and looked at it, wondering how it managed to get into this location.

"I was feeling one of these earlier when we talked about things here that might be a danger. However, what I felt seemed to be distant or hidden, and I could not explain it. Maybe this is it," I said.

"We found two openings into this city, and both had gates with locks on them," he replied.

I asked Mortice, "So far no one has found openings into this city other than the passageway through the mountain and that set of steps we entered with?"

"Not yet. I must wonder how it got in here as I am sure it would need an opening as large as it is, to begin with," he replied.

"We must keep in mind we have seen other wildlife in here as well," I commented.

"Maybe they all climbed up the sides of the mountain and came in that way, but I wish to make sure all the people here are safe," Mortice replied.

"I think we need to make sure a few guards are placed in different areas. We might be able to place a few up on that walkway above us. I don't feel anything, but let's just be sure," I commented.

Mortice called Phil over, showed him what they found, and discussed placing guards in locations that oversaw the entire city. Both gathered a few of the guards around and sent them to different areas in teams. Phil called over to me and asked, "Do you feel anything like this in this city?"

"I don't, but I feel something I can't explain. It's as if I can feel something like that creature, but it seems to be far away or hidden from me in some manner. I think all of us need to find out how that thing and all the other wildlife got into this town."

"I will round up more of the men and ask Nomi to gather up some of his crew so we can start doing a detailed search," Phil replied.

I sent a thought to Ziggy saying, *We need to search around this entire city to find any openings that could allow a metathesis in here, as we just found one dead.*

We have been making the rounds on the edges of this city and have found nothing yet. But we will look a lot closer now that I hear that.

Thank you, I replied.

Mom, would you please ask Carter if she knows of any other openings in this city other than those steps and the passageway?

What's going on?

We just found a beast like the one that attacked Bailey and our pets inside this city. It's dead but had not decomposed, so that means it has found a way in here somehow.

I will see what she thinks.

Thank you.

I received a thought from Bailey: *Your mother just told me you found one of the creatures that attacked us at that one dig. Is it dead?*

Yes, it's dead, but we need to find out how it got in here.

Soon, Steve, Tom, and Art were standing next to me. As we discussed this dead beast, Tom asked, "How did you kill something like that to begin with?"

I looked at Steve, and he was just smiling. Tom and Art looked at him, and Art asked, "Do I dare ask?" Then he started laughing.

"Go on, Steve, tell him what a big mouth you have," I said.

Art looked at Steve, shaking his head, and asked, "Did you kill that beast somehow?"

"I did, as I just opened my mouth and blew it away."

All of us were looking down at it as others from the camp walked up. Most of them were asking, "How long has it been dead?" "Are there more around here?" "Where did it come from?"

I said, "You all have good questions, but you know as much as us. We must find out those answers. First, we need to learn about how this thing managed to enter this city."

One of the excavation crew said, "One thing for sure, this beast may have died within the last few years."

Another group member said, "We have so much to clean out and repair here, and now I wonder if we can get it done and will it be safe."

"Steve, care to open a door and see if you can get Anthony and his crew over here for about a week?"

"That might be a good idea," he replied.

"Why don't you take Max with you, and I will see if we can get some help from our base camp."

"Alright, we'll be back as soon as he can round people up," he replied.

"Steve, let's set up one place for us to enter and exit before we leave," I suggested.

"How about that cleared area that looks like it should be a park?" he asked.

"Sounds good to me," I replied.

"Vanessa, would you care to return to our base camp and get some help?"

"Well, I guess I can, but it might be good if you or someone else joined me," she replied.

"Burdock, would you travel with Vanessa back to our base and see if you can round up some people who can help here?"

"I can do that if you like," he replied.

"You should not be gone long, and we need people here to help clean out the brush and rubble we are dealing with. Also, leave and return to that area that is cleared and looks like a park."

Burdock looked at Vanessa and asked, "Can you do this?"

"Yes, I can. So are you ready?" she asked.

"Let's get it done," he replied.

I looked at everyone around me and said, "Every one of you needs to be very careful because if there is another beast around here like this one, it's extremely dangerous."

CHAPTER 12

Lots of Help

A doorway opened to Lower Etheral. Steve and Max both walked through, and soon that door closed behind them. One more opening became visible, allowing all of us to see our home base camp. Vanessa and Burdock walked through, with it closing behind them.

In Lower Etheral, Max asked Steve, "Where do you think we will find him?"

"Let's walk over to the old town site and see if we can find him over there," Steve replied.

"Anthony, it's good to see you again," Steve said.

Anthony jumped and then turned to find out who had snuck up on him. "Steve, damn, you did that on purpose, didn't you?"

"I have to admit I was quiet."

"Where are the others?"

"About fifteen days away, but we need some major help clearing brush rubble and trees in a mountaintop city we found."

"A city?" he asked.

"Yes, and it seems no one has lived there for centuries, but we need to see if we can make it livable for people who wish to live there."

"Wow. How much time do I have to gather people?"

"We need to return as soon as you can gather some men and women who have the time to help us."

"Wow, just a minute." Then he turned and said to one of the men with him, "Mark, please gather as many people as possible around here who can be gone for a good amount of time and do it fast and get back here. Darnie, please run over to Lower Etheral and see how many men and women want to go with us to an old city on a hill in the western lands."

Both asked at the same time, "What do you want me to ask them?"

"Ask them if they wish to help Marty, Steve, and Bailey on another project further out west."

"Got it, boss, so we meet back here or over in the lot by where they left from last time?"

Steve said, "Let's meet over by that same place we left from last time. We need to leave within, let's say, two hours."

"I will do what I can," Mark replied.

Darnie stated, "Wow, well, I will see what I can do." Then he took off running.

"Anyone up on the hill we need?" Steve asked.

"There are a few, but by the time we ride up there, everyone down here will be ready to go."

"If we open a door up there, will you be able to find them quickly so we can return?" Max asked.

"I can do that if we open up one of those openings you make on the roadway halfway from the top of the mountain to the palace," he replied.

"We can do that, are you ready?" Steve asked.

Looking at Steve with an unsure look on his face, he replied, "I guess so."

Soon a doorway opened, and the three of them walked through it. Once there, Anthony looked around and noticed one of his crew members and ran over to ask him to gather people, saying, "We need anyone who can leave within the next few minutes."

That person ran down the street, knocking on doors, and when someone answered, he spoke to them, then both ran to other homes nearby. Soon about twenty men and women were headed back to join them.

"Is this everyone?" Anthony asked.

"This is all I could round up on short notice."

Steve asked, "Are we ready to go down below?"

"I would have to say yes," Anthony said.

Everyone was looking at each other, and one of them asked, "Go down where?"

With that question asked, Steve created the opening showing them the area we camped in before. As everyone started through, a voice was heard yelling, "Hey, wait for me!" It was a young woman running as fast as she could.

Steve said, "You can slow down. I will wait for you."

"Oh, thank you," she said as she came up almost out of breath.

Soon the group with Steve and Max was near the location everyone had left from the last time our team departed Lower Etheral. Anthony asked one of the guys to go over to Old Etheral and ensure all those people came back and joined us.

All of them were asking, "What are we going to work on?"

Max and Steve started to answer questions while they waited.

As Steve and Max were waiting in Lower Etheral, Vanessa and Burdock had stepped out of their opening at the base camp. People were running around and asking questions, and soon, some of them were rounding up a few who would love to help. They had about fifteen people joining them as they got ready to leave, and a doorway was opened to return.

I was standing there with several of Nomi's crew members as Phil and Mortice walked up. Phil asked, "How soon will others be here to help out?"

"Should be soon as Vanessa just sent a thought saying, 'We are on our way.' As for Steve, I would imagine soon. At least they will be here soon if Steve has not stopped for dinner at that palace."

Suddenly, an opening appeared, and Vanessa was standing there as Burdock walked through with a few from the base camp. Then the breach was gone.

"I need all of you to come over here, please, because there should be another opening soon."

With that area cleared out, I sent Steve a thought, *Are you about ready to come back?*

I am going to open it up now.

Go for it, I said.

Everyone was now looking at another opening, this time with another group of people walking out with Max as Steve was holding the opening. Everyone gathered around after Steve closed his doorway.

Everyone that just arrived was looking all around and speaking of the things they viewed and asking questions, and most of us tried to give them answers. Finally, one of the people from Etheral said, "This is like a jungle here. How are we going to clear all this out?"

"We will do it bit by bit if we must, and yes, we know there is so much brush and growth here. We also realize most of the buildings have trees and vines growing in, through and around them. However, with time and all your help, we will change the look of this place," Steve said.

"OK, I want all of you to work with Nomi and his crew. We have a lot to get done here and not a lot of time to do it in," I said.

Nomi spoke out, saying, "We have machetes for everyone. Shovels, saws, and axes are in that wagon over there." As he was speaking, he pointed to their crew wagon.

Mortice said, "All of you need to see this before you go anyplace." Then he walked over to the dead creature we found with everyone following.

"What the heck is that?" a woman asked.

Phil had walked up and said, "That is one of the deadliest animals you can find in this western region. We don't know how it got inside this city, and we need that answer. However, at the same time, all of you need to keep your eyes and ears open for anything strange."

Nomi said, "All of you will be working with men from my crew and some of the guards, and if you find an opening in the wall or another one of these things, you run like your pants are on fire and yell, so everyone knows."

I said, "In case there is another one of these around, Steve, Art, Tom, and I will take care of it. All of you just need to get a lot of distance from it and maybe hide."

CHAPTER 13

New Finds

Everyone gathered around Nomi, and he started to place two of his men with each group. Mortice added two guards for protection. Soon we had about seven different groups heading to various areas to get rid of the rubble and clear out brush, weeds, and smaller trees on the roadways and paths.

Our mothers were helping Manna and Medina clear out the area they used to cook in earlier. That first meal had been set up in a rough-looking place with lots of dust, dirt, and even brush covering some of the counter areas. Majjeem, Sophia, and Carter were walking around, and I could feel she still had pain but hope. Finally, Vanessa, her sisters, and their pets joined them. All of them started walking in and out of some of the old homes they could enter.

I thought to Vanessa, *Please remember we don't know what is here yet, so all of you be careful. Tell the others as well.*

We will, she replied.

Our pets were walking the outskirts of the city as close to the wall as they could get. They were always looking for that opening.

All of a sudden, I heard Sky bouncing around in my head: *Marty, I don't see your wagon on that path or the road down below. Are all of you safe?*

Just fine, Sky. We are in a town at the very top of this mountain. Most of this city is covered with trees, vines, and other green growth.

Well, let me know if you need us. We will land and get some rest and fly over you tomorrow.

Thank you, Sky. Also, you may wish to keep invisible as we found one of those dead metatheses here.

Did you find one more?

Yes, but it's dead. However, we don't know how it managed to get into this city as there are only two entrances we have found so far.

We will stay alert, and believe me, we will make sure it's cooked if we see one.

Okay, talk later, I said.

Soon, Datilina and Dohadie walked up and asked, "Where are the people from the base camp?"

"Not sure which direction they went. There are Tasha and Meesha. See if they know," I replied as I pointed in their direction. Soon the four of them were walking around, and I noticed Nomi round them up to help.

Marty, we think we found an opening over on the north side of the city.

Not sure which direction that is from here, Ziggy. Can you give me a landmark?

Can you see a building that looks like it has a bell on the top of it?

Standing there looking all around, I soon viewed a large building with what looked like it could be what she was talking about, so I replied, *I think I know what you're talking about, but not sure. So I'm going to get Mortice and Phil and will join you shortly.*

We will be waiting for you, she replied.

"Mortice, can you grab Phil and follow me in that direction?" I pointed toward that tower with the bell in it.

Soon, I was being followed by Mortice, Phil, and several of the guards who were still with them. As we approached Ziggy, Tabby, Agatha, and Masher, they pointed to an opening covered with lots of small trees, brush, and a few rocks. But there was indeed an opening. I sent a thought to Steve asking, *Would you gather Tom and Art and meet over near the tower with the bell? We have found an opening in the wall, it seems.*

71

As we talked about what we could see, Tom, Art, and Steve showed up with Nomi and a few of his men. Along with all of them were Anthony and two of his crew. All of us looked at the opening, and I could feel fear in many of them. But of course, it would not be fair for me to say I didn't feel some fear myself.

I could still feel an animal like the one that was dead, but for some reason, it still felt as though it was hidden or far away. I said, "I can remove most of that rock so we can get through there, but if we are going to do something with those small trees and that brush, we need to be very careful and maybe do that first."

Steve asked me, "Do you feel something that you're not telling me?"

"Why do you ask?" I replied.

"Because I just started to feel something like that beast I killed before."

"I feel it, but I am not sure where it is," I said.

I started lifting the rocks with my power and setting them to the side as others began working on the trees and brush. Within a few hours, we were looking at an area cleared of debris.

CHAPTER 14

A Blast of Fire

I started to walk to that opening, but as I did, I now felt it. As I took a few more steps forward, I could feel that something was inside this tunnel. I know Steve must feel it now as well. It was as if the walls of this tunnel were hiding it from us. I said, "Steve, we have one of those in this tunnel area."

Steve walked up to me and said, "I knew I felt that thing but was not sure why or anything else."

"I think the walls of this tunnel have something that blocks what we feel," I said.

"Does it sense us yet?" he asked.

I walked closer, and suddenly, I said to Steve, "I think it's heading our way."

Steve and I jumped back, and suddenly, my sword was in my hand. Others noticed I was ready to fight, and everyone else readied themselves for battle. Tom changed, and so did Art. Tom was now showing everyone he was Thor, and Art allowed others to see he was not of this world.

All of those around us jumped back, and I am unsure if it was because I pulled my sword or that Tom and Art were now showing all of those around us who they really were.

Within a matter of a few seconds, everyone changed. Our protectors had hands-on weapons, and Steve was moving so no one would be in his way. As we stood there waiting, Tom said, "I sure hope we didn't just show ourselves for no reason at all."

"We have company coming, and when it arrives, it will be deadly, so be prepared."

Steve asked, "It's the same kind of thing I killed before, isn't it?"

"I feel it is, and I know you feel it," I replied.

"I do, and I can feel this one coming toward us," he replied.

"Every one of you should move back as far away from here as you can. We need to make sure and give this thing room as it comes out. It's deadly and takes a lot of power to kill. So all of you move back," I yelled.

Anthony and his crew, along with Nomi and his men, moved back and gave us plenty of room.

Everyone was now standing a great distance behind us and away from that opening. But everyone behind us looked like war was heading in their direction, and they were ready or they were hiding. All at once, something that looked like a metathesis scrambled out of that hole and was moving fast. It was not an elklike creature as I had figured it was from the feeling I was getting.

It was what looked like a snake with four legs and a long tail. It had the scales like the last one we faced. This thing was almost the size of a horse and had claws that looked eight inches in length and were highly deadly. It was tossing out bolts of fire just like that last one did.

All of us tried to maneuver in a position to kill it, but it was swaying back and forth as it seemed to be running like I had seen one of those little lizards back home running across the sand. It was whipping that tail all over the place, and its body was sweeping back and forth like it could jump from one side to the other and not miss a beat.

Many of the guards took a shot at it, and like that last one, they simply bounced off. Art pushed force toward it, and it slowed but not much. Tom raised his hammer, and lightning rose to the sky. Suddenly all the fog was gone and the entire sky lit up with streaks of lightning. We could even see the clouds now.

Lightning was charging that hammer, and Tom brought that hammer down and pointed it at the creature. The tail of the beast thrashed around just as Tom was about to release all that power. Tom's blast of energy was knocked away into the clouds and space as that tail whipped around, blasting his feet out from under him. Steve and I turned and looked at both to make sure they were safe.

It only took a second to return our view to this fast-moving monster headed in our direction. I felt it was just angry but might love to have all of us for dinner. As it came at me, my sword did all the work knocking fire this way and that. I was working overtime to keep up with it. "Steve, can you take this thing out?" I yelled.

"Not with you in the way. Jump to your left and let me handle it," he said.

After he said that, I leaped to my left. As soon as I did, a massive gust of wind blew that creature back against the wall. All at once, that fast-running, swaying, fire-blowing monster turned into a real mess.

Everyone came running over, and all those who just joined us because of the display of power and lightning now saw who Tom and Art really were.

Everyone moved back, and I was getting a feeling from people that they were getting sick. So I said, "All of you who can't handle this mess, please walk away now."

Steve said, "It's a good thing you yelled when you did because I was wondering if I would have a clear shot at it."

Tom and Art were both dusting themselves off, and Tom said, "I think I just got knocked down by a big lizard."

Art said, "That wasn't just a lizard. That was power and fire wrapped in lots of protection."

Tom asked, "Steve, are you planning on cleaning up this mess you made?" Then he laughed.

Everyone was laughing, but I stopped and stood there as if listening and then spoke out, saying, "All of you may wish to back farther as I feel that's not the only one. I feel one more someplace in that tunneled-out area."

Everyone backed up far enough to make sure they could run if need be. Tom, Steve, Art, and I backed up but stood and waited. "Do you feel it's headed our way?" Tom asked.

I stood there for a moment, then slowly walked up toward the opening. "No, actually, I believe it's moving away," I replied.

Steve said, "I feel the same thing about whatever it is. It would be nice to know where this tunnel area goes and, of course, where it ends on the outside of this wall."

I started to walk up closer to the opening and still felt that beast, but it was as if it was now running for its life. I turned and asked if someone could get a few torches. One of Anthony's group took off running, saying, "I will find a few."

As all of us were waiting, I noticed a pipeline running through this tunnel, along the floor. As I looked at it more, I started to wonder what it was.

"Notice that pipe running through this tunnel?" I asked no one specifically.

Nomi walked up and looked at it and asked, "What do you think it is?"

I replied, "We found a good water source almost in the center of this city, but now I am wondering if they set up sewer lines for all of these homes and buildings as well."

Steve commented, "These people seem to have achieved a good number of things way back then that most other areas still haven't."

One of the men ran up almost out of breath and said, "I found three of them."

"OK, let's light them up and find out what this is and where it goes."

"What about that thing in there?" one of the men asked.

"If it's still in there, it won't be for long," I said.

Nomi walked up to me, and I could feel his fear, but he asked, "Do you want me to take the lead on this one?"

I looked at him, just gave him a huge smile almost laughing, and then I asked, "You really wish to take the lead on this one?"

"If you need me to, I sure will," he replied.

I was starting to feel he was very uncomfortable with that idea, so I said, "I know you are willing to lead, but I feel we need to have power in the lead just in case we run into more than one of those creatures. So, I will do the honors this time, but thank you for the offer."

I could feel him calm down and relax as I said that.

"No problem, I'd be glad to do it if you would like, but I was hoping you would say that."

"Nomi, I appreciate the offer, but I can't afford to lose you to some beast."

He looked at me, and I could tell he was feeling proud.

CHAPTER 15

More Than One

I took a torch and started to go into the passageway. It was about five feet wide and around six feet in height, so there was not a big problem with walking space. The floor was clear, and the pipe was lying in a groove of a kind. The rest of the surface was like a bed of gravel. Now and again, we found large sections of rock that must have dislodged from the walls or ceiling and ended up in our way. I turned and stated, "Tom, I know you're back there."

"I am. What do you need, Marty?"

"I need a really big hammer." Then I started laughing.

Soon he was standing near me and said, "I see what you mean."

"Looks like that beast's tail was knocking a lot of things loose and I just don't want anything in our way in case we need to get back fast," I stated.

"I think we can handle this." So he gave the hammer a slight swing, and the rock was soon in tiny pieces.

"Wow, you hardly took a swing at that thing," I said.

"Oh, I know. It's amazing what this can do. I am shocked I didn't take out a wall when that thing knocked me for a loop."

"Well, I'm glad you didn't," I replied.

We must have walked for a good ten minutes, and I felt that beast again, but this time, it was not moving. Steve was right behind Tom and started to ask, "Marty—"

Before he could say another word, I said, "I know, Steve."

"How far ahead of us is it?" Tom asked.

"I would have to say not far at all," I replied.

"Do you want me to take the lead?" Steve asked.

"I think I can have my power ready this time, but just in case, you may wish to trade places with Tom so you can look over my shoulder."

Tom asked, "Do you feel that thing nearby?"

"I do," I replied.

I was now feeling more than one, but the other two felt more like they were young. I said, "I have a feeling that the one we killed was protecting his family."

"His family?" Steve asked.

"Can you sense more than one?" I asked.

We stopped for a moment so he could focus on his feelings, and suddenly he said, "I think you're correct, buddy. So what do we do with Mom and the kids?"

"I'm not sure, to be honest with you. Those babies will grow up to be just as dangerous as the others we have faced. Maybe I can pick all of them up, and we can carry them out to the end of wherever this tunnel goes." I commented.

"What if it goes no place but a significant drop-off or hole in the ground? That thing will be spitting fire all the time you are trying to protect it," Steve said.

While we stood there, I thought, *Can you move your babies out of here? I wish you could understand me. I don't want to kill you.*

I didn't hear anything, so I tried one more time. *I don't want to hurt or kill you.*

I started getting a different kind of feeling. Before, I felt fear and anger, but now much of that anger was going away.

Steve spoke up and said, "Something I am feeling has changed, and I am not sure what it is."

"I have that same feeling. It's as though she's not angry now. But she still has a fear of us. So I am trying to speak to her."

I thought again, *I don't want to kill you or hurt you and your babies. Please let me help you.*

Steve said, "Marty, she's coming this way."

"I feel that Steve."

"Don't you think we need to get out of here?" he asked.

I said, "Tom, would you please take anyone behind you back to the entrance and make sure everyone is away from the entrance."

He replied, "What about the two of you?"

"I feel we will be fine."

Steve said, "Marty, what are you talking about? This thing is coming to kill us."

I replied, "You don't know that."

Steve and I stood there as both of us could feel her approaching. As we stared into the opening in front of us, we were limited on how far we could see. But we knew she was close, and I thought, *We can help you if you allow us.*

Then in the darkness, our torches gave us a glimpse of eyes, and those eyes kept moving toward us. Now I was thinking of how people in this world react to our powers. I didn't bother to hide them, and I told Steve, "You need to relax. You know I understand what you're feeling. What if she understands that as well?"

I started to feel Steve calm down and slow his breathing. Soon he had lost his fear of her.

She kept advancing as both of us stood there. Soon she was within ten feet of us, and I thought, *We can help you if you let us. We are not from your world.*

She tipped her head like I used to see Ziggy do as a pup when she was trying to understand me. I reached out with my hand, and she came closer. I thought again, *I know you can feel my power as others do in your world, but do not be afraid.*

As I was standing there with my arm and hand extended, this creature placed her nose against my hand, and when she did, she reacted, but it wasn't the old shake, rattle, and rock. Instead, it was more like a murmur, and her entire body reverberated, then she took a step back.

Steve said, "I think she is trying to speak to you."

"What do you mean? Can you understand her as you did with those trumps?"

"I'm not sure, but it seems she said something, and I didn't understand it."

"Talk to her, Steve, and tell her we do not wish to harm her or her babies."

Chapter 16

A New Life

I stood there watching her move this way and that, turning now and again to look at Steve to see what he was doing. Finally, I leaned up against the tunnel wall and waited to hear about what was happening. As I was not paying attention, I suddenly felt something bump into me, and I jumped. Then it dawned on me she had placed her nose against my side to get my attention.

Steve said, "She believes we can help her and the babies. She is willing to do whatever it takes to keep them safe."

"Did you ask her where this tunnel goes to?"

"She says it used to go out to the forest. But rocks fell and closed that way out."

"I wonder if we can blast that open," I said.

I had the feeling Tom was coming our way, so I said to Steve, "Stop Tom and tell him we are doing just fine. He's headed our way now."

Steve was quiet for a moment, then left. As he walked away, I watched, and soon I felt him returning and Tom walking away.

"Alright Steve, what do we do?"

"She asked if she could stay here."

"Steve, there is no food for her here. Ask her if we open a doorway to the area past the mountains out west, would she leave and not bother people again?"

After a few minutes of quiet, Steve spoke up, saying, "She would like that."

"Good, tell her to stay here. I need to find someone that has been out to that area. I must know what to look for when I open the door."

As I walked back outside, I sent a thought to Medina asking, *Have you ever seen the forests out west past the mountain ranges?*

I have been there often. It's a jungle of sorts and not a place for men to travel to as most of the area is only for wildlife, and I mean very deadly wildlife.

Can a metathesis live there? I asked.

I know they have many there if that's what you mean. But you also need to know this is not a metathesis as it's a relative of those called a metathalan, she stated.

But they are closely related, correct? I asked.

Yes, they are, and I guess they could be cousins.

I need to get a vision of a place to allow this mother and her babies to have a place to live.

I don't know how to show you my views, Medina replied.

I may know of a way to find that out, I replied.

Vanessa, I need your assistance to see a location that someone has seen in the far west lands.

Vanessa walked up and asked, "Do you want to open an event so these creatures can pass out of this area and into that far region?"

"That's what I want," I replied.

She said, "I can find out from someone who has been there if that's what you need."

"That is what I need, and Medina has seen that part of this region a number of times."

She walked over to Medina and then said, "I need you to think of that area for me." Then she reached out and touched her, not on her head, but simply placed her hand on her shoulder. As she did, both jumped a bit, and then I felt both just connected. Medina said, "My, how your powers have grown, young one."

Soon, Vanessa stepped back, turned, and looked at me, then walked over to where I stood.

"Can you see what she sees?" I asked.

"I could see what it is we need, and I can open that doorway if you want me to," she replied.

"Vanessa, this creature will scare you to death if you see her, so you need to understand that."

As I was saying that, Vanessa reached out and touched me. She suddenly jumped, saying, "Dear lords." I felt her fear, but soon, it was gone. She said, "I understand now, so we need to open this door from just inside that entrance so others will not see her and become afraid."

Both of us started walking back to the entrance. Others were all asking questions, and Tom and Art were standing there with Tom asking, "Did you communicate with her?"

"I didn't, but Steve did."

"So, all of you are going to be safe?" he asked.

"Yes," I replied. Then Vanessa and I walked into the entrance.

I turned and spoke, "All of you need to move far away from this entrance, and please do it now." Then I turned to Vanessa and said, "Alright, let's open it up, and I will look and see what it's like."

Suddenly an opening was in front of us. I walked out to see what was there. I walked around the opening and could see a jungle in front of me with mountains behind me. I walked back inside and said, "Thank you, let's close it now. We need to be sure those babies are at her side. So you stay here. I'm not sure how long it will take for her to collect her babies. I will be back soon with Momma and her babies. Then we will open that doorway again."

Steve, tell her I am coming back, and we need to gather the babies up and bring them with us. Explain to her we are going to open a doorway to the far west so she can find a new home.

When I returned to where Steve was, I found a surprise. Three little surprises were sitting next to their mother in front of Steve. I looked at all of them and noticed the little ones were in no way close to as scary as the mother or their father was. So I said to Steve, "If we are ready, let's move them all out. Vanessa is going to open the doorway."

He looked at me and asked, "Vanessa? Do you realize what she will do when she sees her? Marty, she is going to freak out."

"Calm down. Vanessa already knows how she looks. I am not going into how she knows at this time. But all of us need to move now."

As he was quiet for a few minutes, I felt something that gave me a reason to believe Momma was happy and grateful now. Steve looked at me and said, "She is ready."

As I turned and started walking, I felt all of them behind, traveling in the same direction. Soon I spoke out and said, "Vanessa, I think it's time."

When I said that, she opened the doorway, and all of us walked forward. I walked out into the new land. Steve followed me with four metathalans behind him. All of us were now standing in the far western region.

I watched as she walked out and looked all over with her little ones behind her. Then, she walked around and looked behind the opening to see what was there as well.

Steve said, "I think she likes this area over where she was."

"That's good," I replied.

We watched as the babies started running around and playing. I was standing looking at them. Then, I felt her coming toward me. She nudged me with her nose, and I turned and placed my hand on her head. As I did, she seemed to lower her head. Steve said, "She will always remember how we helped her and the little ones."

I told Steve, "Make sure she understands she scares people, so she needs to avoid all of them."

"She said what I think means, 'Thank you.'" Steve stated.

"Tell her to be safe and have a good life."

We watched as all of them walked off into the jungle we were facing.

Vanessa asked, "Are we ready to return now?"

As I looked at Steve, he nodded his head yes, and I said, "Yes, it's time."

So back through the opening we walked, and Vanessa closed it.

Chapter 17

Questions and Answers

As the doorway closed, we were viewing the faces of everyone in our camp. Then, someone said, "We could not even see all of you."

Vanessa said, "That's good because if you could have seen what was with us, most of you would have run, screamed, and found a place to hide. We didn't want to scare you."

Tom asked, "What did you do with her?"

"It was not just her as she had three little ones. Vanessa opened a door to the lands beyond the mountains west of here, and they walked out to a new life."

Steve said, "I learned today why I have never wanted to kill anything. They simply wished to be left alone, and the one that came out and attacked us was simply protecting his family. I have to say, now that I understand that, I feel bad that I had to kill those babies' father."

Bailey said, "Steve, the two of you saved the others and set them free, and that has to mean something."

"It does, Bailey, but after getting to know her and talking with her . . . I mean I was actually talking to her like I talked to those trumps. I have always felt like Marty, never wanting to harm living creatures, but now I have."

I said, "Sometimes I wish we had the power to stop or go back in time."

Steve added, "I have to agree with you on this one."

Steve and I walked back over to the entrance, and I said, "Well, let's find out where this goes."

I looked around for a few torches, and one of Nomi's men was nearby and saw me looking around. Then he asked, "Are you looking for one of these?"

"I am looking for at least two of those and a match if you have one."

"Here you go," he said as he handed us two lit torches.

"Thank you," I replied.

Art walked up to us and asked Steve and me both, "What if you could stop, and go back in time? What would you do?"

Steve turned and looked at him, and so did I, but it was Steve who spoke out, saying, "If I could change what just happened, I would."

"Let's walk," Art said.

Soon the three of us were walking through the tunnel area and finally found the end. As I was standing there, I asked Steve, "Do you think we can give enough power to blow all this rubble out?"

"I'm not sure, but I think we can give it a try," he replied.

"Art, you might wish to stand back a bit on this."

Steve and I both gave that last part of that tunnel enough power to open it up, and soon the three of us were looking out over the edge of a section of the mountain that had a smell of its own. I turned to Steve and Art, saying, "Maybe we should close this off so that smell will not reach back inside, and of course, no beasts can enter."

Art replied, "You may have an excellent idea about that one."

Steve said, "You know that pipe is still out there, and we could fill this opening again."

"It might be a great idea," I replied.

Soon we were using some of our power to damage the upper section of the entrance to make sure it fell and closed off that opening. The three of us were shaking our heads, and Art said, "You know it's a good thing all of that was not new because we might have been dealing with a gas and fire situation."

As we walked back through the tunnel to reach the city again, Art said, "This city thanks you for closing that off."

Then the three of us just laughed.

As we walked out, we looked around and noticed no one was standing near us, and Art asked, "What would you do if you could go back in time?"

Steve and I looked at each other, and this time I spoke out, saying, "As Steve commented earlier, if we could go back in time and prevent what happened, I would like to see that, but we know we can't do that."

"What if I could make that happen? With both of you standing in front of that opening like you were earlier today. Standing there before that beast came out. Giving you the chance to change events and protect that beast and his family before all the events took place?"

"I would do that in a heartbeat," Steve said.

"I would too," I replied.

CHAPTER 18

A Different Time

*Marty, we think we found an opening over on the north side
of the city.*

Ziggy, is that you?

Yes, we have found an opening, so what do you want us to do?

Are you near the building with the bell in it?

We are, Ziggy replied.

Do me a favor, and you and everyone with you leave that area now.

OK, she replied.

I turned and looked at Steve, then both of us stood there looking
all around at everything and everyone. Then I said, "We are back in
time, and we need to get over to that opening and start communicating,
or we repeat what happened last time."

"I knew there was something weird here," Steve replied.

"Nomi, would you please find a few people who can go with us
to help clear an entrance to a tunnel? We will also need two torches
and a few matches."

"Come with me. I'll get them," he replied.

"Thank you," I said.

"So where are you going that you will need those?"

"Not sure we will need them but just in case, as there are plenty
of places here that are dark."

"Here are two men to help you clear that area you need to be cleared," he stated.

"Thank you," I replied.

"Well, give me a yell if you need more help," he said.

Steve said, "We will."

"OK, what do we do?" Steve asked.

"The very first thing we have to do is get that entrance cleared out enough so we can get inside it," I replied.

"Before you started to communicate with the mother, I was talking to her, telling her we are not from this world, and we can help her."

"Well, I guess you better start trying to talk to her now and tell her to have her mate contact me so that he won't die," Steve said.

I hope you can understand me because I am not from this world, and I don't wish to see you and your young ones killed. After saying that, I looked at Steve and asked him, "Anything?"

"Not yet but keep trying. Maybe the reason it's not working yet is because of the way that tunnel blocked them from us before."

"Anything is possible, I guess," I replied.

Walking up to that entrance, I noticed Ziggy, Masher, and Agatha standing there. So we walked up to them, and I said, "Ziggy, I told you to make sure all of you were nowhere close to this spot."

"We know, Marty, but we feel you might need us on this one."

"We will be fine, Ziggy. I need all of you as far away from this opening as possible. Please understand, Steve and I already know what we need to do. We don't want anyone else to know about it," I stated.

"Well, but you make sure to yell if you need us," she replied.

"Thank you, Ziggy," I answered.

"Steve, let's continue. I will start sending my thoughts again and see if I can reach them," I said.

We are not from your world, and I don't wish to kill you or harm you or your babies. So please try to understand what it is I am saying.

Can you understand me? I do not want to harm your babies or you.

Do you understand me? Please try to understand what I am saying because I can save you and your babies.

"Anything at all yet?" I asked.

"I heard something but was not sure what it was," he replied.

I said, "You made that same remark the last time she contacted you, so talk to them." I replied.

I said again, *Can you hear me? If you can please speak to us so we can keep you alive, do you understand?*

Suddenly, Steve nudged me and shook his head, so I stopped what I was saying.

"I am speaking with the male, it seems, and I said we would like to walk in and allow him to feel our power."

"So, what did he say back?"

"He said the entrance is blocked with rocks and trees. So it might be hard for us to enter."

I replied, "Just tell him we're gods and can overcome such little obstacles."

Steve looked at me and asked, "You're not letting this god thing go to your head, are you?"

"No, but it just seems that's the easiest way to get people here to let us help them," I exclaimed.

"Seems you're correct, I will tell him we are clearing the way and can move him and his family to a new and better place to live," Steve stated.

I turned and looked at the two men from Nomi's crew and asked if they would give us a hand clearing the way. They cut down brush and branches, and I removed many of the rocks by simply picking them up and tossing them aside.

Soon most of the work was complete, and Steve looked at Nomi's men, saying, "Hey, guys, great job, thank you, but now just in case, we want you both to be safe and move far away from this entrance."

I could feel the creature near that opening, and I was still working on removing debris so we could enter, then I figured they could meet us. As I was clearing the way, most of my power was in the open, and he could feel all of it. Finally, I got to the point where there was enough room for both of us to walk through. I asked Steve, "Well, are we on good terms so far?"

"I think you have already convinced him you're not from this world. He is ready to leave this place if we can help him and his family," Steve said.

"Please ask him if we can enter," I replied.

"He said yes."

I picked up two torches and used a match to light them, then handed one to Steve, and I started to walk in. All the time I had been standing out here or clearing this area, I felt changes in this creature. At first, it was hostility and anger, then it seemed to mellow out a bit, and slowly it was a feeling of hope.

I mentally said, *I look forward to helping you and your family find a better place to live.*

Thank you suddenly rang inside my head.

Did you just communicate with me?

Yes, I did, and my family and I will never forget who you are and what it is you are doing.

Steve will stand at the entrance, then he is going to create an opening that all of us can walk through to your new home. But we need your partner and babies as well before we can leave.

They are coming now, he replied.

I am pleased you and I can speak. I have never wished to harm any life form, and I am pleased we can help you today.

I was looking around as he was standing in front of me. Then suddenly, I noticed movement around him and viewed the babies once again.

My parents always told me that the most precious thing in the world is our children, and as I view yours, I see love and happiness.

We are ready anytime you are, he said.

"Steve, open it up. Let's move them out of this place," I said.

Within a moment's time, an opening appeared that gave us the view we had seen earlier in the day. As Steve kept it open, I walked out into the new area of the region and looked around. I viewed behind the opening and made sure it was safe. Then I motioned for them to follow me.

Soon an enormous lizard-looking creature was passing by me and looking all around, then he turned and made a few noises. His family followed him into their new home area.

I wish you well, and please stay away from people here as they are terrified of how you look.

We will, and thank you, he replied.

Steve and I were now watching as the babies were running around, and all I could feel was happiness and excitement.

Suddenly, I felt the female walking up to me. With her nose, she got my attention. I placed my hand on her head. Then I heard her say, *Thank you,* and they all turned around and walked into the jungle area.

I walked back through the doorway and looked at Steve, and he was nodding his head as if to say yes. Then the opening closed. Both of us noticed one person sitting on a huge rock in front of us. As we walked forward, I said, "That was amazing and wonderful. Thank you."

Steve looked at him and commented, "To me, that was one of the greatest things we could have done—to save that entire family and allow them to start their lives in a location suited to them."

Art stood up and said, "The two of you have shown me how much you both respect the lives of any other living creature. I am proud of you both."

Steve said, "Marty has always felt there are better ways to work things out than harming or killing anything."

"Well, both of you now understand no one knows anything about what happened before we changed that situation," Art stated.

"People will still know who you and Thor are, as they saw all the lightning and both of you change," I replied.

"Maybe not," Steve replied.

Art continued with what Steve said by adding, "All those other events never happened now."

Steve and I looked at each other, and he was nodding his head, grinning from ear to ear, saying, "That is what I was wondering."

"Wow, all of that now really seems strange," I said.

"Just don't mention to Tom how he lit up the sky," Art said.

"So, I can't tell him I saw him in action?" I asked.

"Not a good idea," Art stated.

Both Steve and I nodded our heads in agreement, and I said, "You're correct—that would not be good."

CHAPTER 19

Creating A Community

"Hey, Marty, what was in that passageway we found?" Ziggy asked.

"There is a pipe that runs through there, and I figured it must be a drain for sewage," I replied.

"Do you think we should check it out because we still are not sure how that beast entered this place if there is no other opening?"

Steve sent me a thought asking, *Do we need to get back over there and open that up again and close it?*

I replied, *I'm not sure, but maybe it might be a good idea to put all questions to rest.*

I said to Ziggy, "I got the feeling it was just closed on the other end. But I guess we could look."

Ziggy, Masher, Agatha, Steve, and I started walking over to the opening, and Art walked over and asked, "Where are you heading?"

"Our pets want to make sure that the tunnel is not open on the other end. So all of us are going to see what's there," I replied.

"Oh, don't worry about it. I walked through that and found the other end open. It stunk so bad from waste I created a little rockslide and covered the end of that tunnel. So that smell will not come back in here, but that pipe is still in place to allow the sewage to run out. I guess that could have been the way that beast entered here. But now that we found that, we should not see any more of those," Art said.

Ziggy said, "Well, I guess we have our answer about how he got in here."

"Well, if all of you wish to continue searching the area, it might still be a good idea," Steve added.

"That's true because there may very well be more openings around here as we have seen more wildlife here lately, but be sure not to take any chances. If you find something, please be sure to let me know," I declared.

Everyone seemed busy clearing out areas and even cutting down a few of the trees that had grown up through paths and homes. With the two new groups we rounded up and all those we had with us previously, we could now see some buildings we could not see before. Maybe in a month or two, with this kind of help, people could start to view a little town again.

Anthony walked up with two others and asked me, "Marty, if we can get this place all cleaned up and the brush and debris cleared out, can people live here again?"

"I don't know why not, but I think what we need to do is wait and see if we can bring back Zane, Carter's love. If the two of them wish to stay here, people might have the magic to protect them, but I guess we will see what happens. Anubis is still searching for him," I commented.

"That would be great if some of us could move out here and create lives in this part of the land," Anthony said.

"I think everyone needs to make sure that those vines, brush, and trees that are covering everything get removed first. But who knows? If it's all cleaned up and set up again, it might be an excellent place to settle down," Steve commented.

One of the men with Anthony said, "I have never seen any place that had so much growing on the buildings, and it's almost like you can't see the sky for the branches and vines. However, many of us think if it's all cleaned up with places to live, as you say, this might be a good place to start a new life."

I could feel the excitement in the two who were with him and in Anthony himself. I sensed that a few of them would love to move out this way and rebuild this place.

I spoke out and commented, "If people come out here to live, they will have to be creative. They will have to make things to sell in other places or trade them for items they would need."

Anthony and his men were nodding, and Anthony replied, "It seems all the people who lived here before must have done that, as they built this entire city. So I would imagine many more people could do it again."

Replying, I said, "That is very true, but keep in mind, Etheral is not as close as an open door."

As Steve, Art, and I walked around and spoke to people, we found many people might wish to settle down here. Even some of the excavation crew asked if it would be possible.

I guess those in the excavation crew could be close to where they needed to search and have family close to them. Some people talked about going up to that walkway and finding a place they could climb out with a rope around them and cut down trees that were blocking the views.

Groups of people were all over the place. Some of those in the excavation crew often would yell, "Look at this." Others were shouting, "What a find." But it all seemed to be an exciting group as even those finding wonderful new treasures were clearing places and helping all the others who needed help.

"How about a hand over here?" one person would yell.

Then suddenly, many voices yelled back, "Where are you?"

After those voices found out where that person needed help, all of them rushed over to see what they could do. It was a new community of people all working to help each other in any way they could.

Steve and Bailey walked up to me with Steve saying, "I find it amazing how all these people work to help each other despite the color of skin, size, or belief."

"Could you imagine what it would be like if all racists back home stopped acting as if they were better than others and cared about the human race along with its survival?" Bailey asked.

"I can, and everyone must keep in mind back home that racism is not just one group of people. I know for the most part many can't see past the color on their nose, we must keep in mind that can be seen in every race on earth." I declared.

"Do you think it will ever change?" Bailey asked.

"What is needed is all people must learn to accept each other as human beings. Everyone should remember we all have faults, may speak differently, look different, act different, and even have educational dysfunctions of one kind or another to some degree," I replied.

Bailey stated, "It would be fantastic if people on our planet worked as these people do at helping others. Can you imagine all the accomplishments men and women could make happen back home?"

"I know people today on Earth could already be exploring new worlds and the universe. But because of hate for their fellow men and women, they allow the greatest achievements that can be created to be lost for all time," I declared.

As we stood there speaking about how we thought our own world could change, I got the feeling there was trouble, and suddenly someone yelled, "Help!"

Looking around, we noticed people running to the west side of the town, so we joined them. On the way, Art and Tom joined us. Tom asked, "What do you think it is?"

"No idea yet, but we will soon see, I am sure," I said.

Everyone was running around a large building and suddenly stopped. All of us ran up and almost ran into many of those who came to an abrupt halt. People had been cutting down a few of the trees that had grown up through homes. In front of us was one of those trees. One person was now hanging upside down on a rope from about halfway up.

"Please move aside, people, so we can help him," Steve yelled.

We walked up, and we told all of those around us, "Relax, we will get him down."

Soon, he stopped screaming and waving his arms around, and Steve, Bailey, and I walked forward with Art and Tom behind us. He was hanging about twenty feet from the ground, so Steve and I walked up under him, looked at each other, and started to grow in height. Many who never saw us do that before were just standing there in amazement with heart-stopping looks on their faces.

As we reached him, I noticed his eyes were wide open, with a surprised look on his face. I said, "We are going to raise you so you can untangle yourself first, then place you on that section of the tree that looks safe." I pointed at what was a substantial open space between the larger branches.

He was trying to speak, but the words that came out seemed to be all garbled at first, then he managed to gain control and replied, "Thank you."

As I raised the man in the air, it was as if an invisible hand was under him. Steve reached out and unwound the rope that had wrapped around him. Then with all the line now hanging free, Steve gathered it, and as I placed the man in a large section of the tree that offered him a safe location, Steve handed him all the rope.

Some of those on other branches of that tree all shouted and started to cheer. It wasn't long before the people on the ground started cheering and clapping.

"Do you need more help? Are you and those with you going to be able to finish this safely?" I asked.

"I feel we can finish this safely. I was just not paying attention to where I stepped," he replied.

Steve added, "There is no need to take unnecessary chances at making this city livable again. There are many of us here who can help."

"Time to rock and roll, you're now on your own again," I said.

Then as Steve looked over at me, he sent a thought saying, *Good job, Batman.* Then as we both were becoming our normal size again, Steve and I were laughing.

Bailey was standing there as we were laughing, just shaking her head, looking down at Ziggy, saying, "Another inside joke."

We were both still laughing about what Steve said. Then I asked, "So, does that make you the boy wonder Robin and Bailey, Batwoman?"

Steve replied, "No matter what, we have always been a great team."

Bailey said, "We have, we are, and always will be a great team with our protectors."

Both Steve and I shook our heads, with Steve replying, "You got it, Batwoman."

Art and Tom were both standing there with unique looks on their faces. They had been watching, and now that we were back on the ground, they walked up with Art asking, "Well, you showed us that trick two times now. Is there a lot more you can do that we will see soon?"

"I don't know until the time other powers are needed," I replied.

Bailey said, "We have surprised ourselves many times, as things happen as they need to."

Steve added, "Most of our powers came to us when danger arrived."

Manna yelled out, "If you want to eat, you better beat feet and get over here."

People headed to where everything had been cleaned, now a great place to cook and eat. Anthony and his crew, those from our base camp, and Nomi's crew found a plate and utensils and got in line. Of course, our team was there as well. Several people were dishing out what looked like meat and beans.

I figured the meat could have been from that wild boar the men got the previous day, but now I was wondering how many cans of beans they had brought, so I asked Manna, "How many cans of beans did we bring with us?"

Her reply was, "Cans of beans? We didn't bring any cans of beans at all, Marty. Do you see those big sacks on that wagon over there?" Then she pointed to the closest cart.

"Those are all beans?" I asked.

Manna replied, "All of those big sacks are loaded with beans."

"So are you soaking them in water and then cooking them up?" I asked.

"Yes, it works out very well as we have a lot of mouths to feed," she stated.

"Well, if you find anything you need, all you must do is ask, and one of us can take you back to Etheral if you like," Bailey said.

Nomi stood up on a stool and asked, "Do all of you have what you need for tools? If you don't, let me know because we have many more in our wagons."

A few spoke out about things they could use, and Nomi told them, "Meet up with me after eating."

Carter was sitting with our mothers. I walked over with Bailey and sat down. She looked at me and asked, "Have you heard anything yet?"

"I have, and he said he is doing a lot of soul-searching. I believe if it is possible, he will make it happen," I replied.

"He is searching for souls?" she asked.

"That's what he said, and that was this morning," I said.

"I just keep hoping it will happen, but at the same time, I am trying not to get my hopes up too much," she commented.

Bailey said, "I can understand that completely. So what have you been doing to keep your mind off those kinds of things?"

Carter said, "I have been working on my home but finding it's not easy to get things back to what it was at one time. I had to have a few come over and cut down a huge tree that grew up in one of the rooms. I found that room will never be used for anything, even with most of that tree removed."

Anthony spoke out and asked, "Why not let all of us build you a new home? There are a lot of old buildings falling, damaged, or just rotted that we could remove, and we could build new homes in their place."

She looked over at him and replied, "That might be the way to go. What I once had is not the same today."

A few others started to discuss that idea. Finally, one of the men from our base camp said, "One thing for sure, there are many trees that should be removed, leaving those that add to the beauty."

Another man added, "I have heard many trees are growing outside this city. Maybe some of those could be cut, trimmed, and taken back to our mill. Then we could cut the wood to size and create homes like the ones we are building there."

Steve said, "That's true as we must simply cut them and load them on a wagon and open a doorway. Then the crews back there could work their magic."

I said, "We need to set up a way to move them other than a wagon, I think, because some of these are trees of great size."

People were getting excited about building new homes. I thought many of the old structures were going to be demolished, as Anthony stated. So building something new in its place would be good.

Some of the people were starting to speak about building new homes here and moving out here. So I asked Carter, "What would you think of having some of these people moving out here to live?"

She replied, "I think it would be wonderful to see this town come to life one more time."

CHAPTER 20

Creating Ideas

"What we need to do is get rid of all those vines and brush then tackle those trees," Nomi commented.

Mortice said, "I must agree with you on that because all that coverage would make it difficult to move any trees."

I replied, "I can have Sky and Jasmin make a pass or two over this town and burn off a lot of that on top of those trees and buildings. We would have to make sure we don't end up with lots of fires we didn't want, however."

Nomi said, "Maybe one pass over the entire town because we just need to see about getting the vines off the top."

"We will need to have everyone ready to put out fires if they start, just in case," Steve added.

Sky, can you make a pass over the top of this town and only burn off the vines that cover the trees and buildings? I asked.

Marty, I can fly low and try to burn off only those vines and hope I don't do more damage, she replied.

All right, just one pass to see how that works, but let me warn the people first, I replied.

It will be a short time as we are flying around and will be back in a bit, she stated.

I stood up on top of a huge tree that had been cut down and was now on a path ready to go to the mill. I yelled so everyone could hear me, saying, "I need everyone to take cover and then watch for fires. I am having our two friends fly over and burn off the vines on the top of everything."

Art and Tom looked at me and Tom asked, "How are you making that happen?"

Steve spoke, saying, "He was just communicating with them and asked them to make a pass over us and burn off the top."

Everyone, including Nomi, was looking at one another, then started looking up to see if there was a fire in the sky.

Sky, I think we are ready but don't burn down the city, I said.

Suddenly, two dragons were flying over us, and I noticed they were not blasting out flames like I had seen them do before. They seemed to be shooting out smaller flames to remove the greenery on top of everything.

As they passed over us, cheering and yelling started to take place all over this city, with people saying to others, "Look at that," "Did you see that?" "That was great." "Wow," and I could feel all the love for our two friends right now so much.

Everyone was now looking up at a sky with clouds and could see them—something they could not view before.

Thank you, Sky, I said.

Oh, you are very welcome, and we didn't burn anything important, I hope.

You did just great, and I could feel the love from all these people down here for both of you as you two flew over. Thank you, I replied.

"All right, I guess we are ready to get back to work," Nomi stated.

"Yes, we need to figure out where we are going to place all the cut trees. They must have the branches cut off as well," Anthony declared.

I spoke out saying, "That would be a good idea because they need only the main sections of the tree. I would, however, suggest making sure all the overgrowth is removed first."

Then Nomi added, "We must clear good paths. Then we need to tag trees that we are going to cut down and remember which way we want them to fall."

Art said, "Many of the people here think we need to cut down the trees on that outside cliff area. That seems like a good idea as those trees would end up in a huge pile at the bottom of the mountain."

Steve said, "I think we need to find people who know what it's like to cut trees because we recently noticed not everyone knows how to do that safely."

Tom spoke out, saying, "Well, only one way to find out is to ask. So let's gather everyone around, and Nomi, you can do the honors of finding our real tree cutters."

"We call them lumbermen and lumberjacks at home. They are people who work with cutting down trees and transporting them," I articulated.

Nomi said, "Well, I will ask if we have any lumber . . . what?"

"They are called lumberjacks," Bailey replied.

"Right, I will yell, 'Are there any lumberjacks in the crowd?' and see if that gets their attention. Then, after all of them are looking at me, wondering what the heck I just asked, I will ask them again if anyone knows how to cut down trees."

"I think if they are going to be cutting trees on that cliff area, they need to start down toward the bottom of the hill. That way, the trees above them will fall to the bottom instead of getting caught up in a big cluster that people can get killed in," I stated.

"Well, we need lots of rope, it seems, and harnesses, and we don't have that here," Nomi stated.

"We can take care of that when the time comes," I replied.

"Steve, we may be heading back to Etheral and contacting the king and finding out if we can get as much rope as possible."

"You know he will want to come out here and see all this," he replied.

"Well, let's gather everyone up and ask the questions," Nomi said.

I climbed up on a tall rock and spoke out in a booming voice again, "We need everyone over here, please."

As we waited, we discussed how we could cut those trees on that cliff face. Steve said, "You know, I could probably blow all of those down to the bottom, and then we would just have to have people cut them up."

I said, "That is an idea that might work. However, I am not sure how much dirt will be removed from them as they are blown down the hill. And I'm not sure how much wind it will take."

Bailey said, "We could always give it a shot and see if it will work."

I said, "Well, I guess I could hold him out above the edge and let him try, but what happens if I can't hold him, and he blows himself into space?"

"Hilarious, Marty," Steve commented.

People started gathering around, and soon it looked like everyone was with us. Nomi found a place to stand and spoke out, saying, "We need to know . . ." Then he stopped and looked at me and asked, "What was that you called them?"

"You mean lumberjacks?" I replied.

"Oh, yes." Then he continued to ask, "We need to know if we have any lumberjacks here."

Lots of people were looking around, shaking their heads, and wondering, "What the heck is that?" He knew he had their attention and asked again, "We need to know if we have any experienced tree cutters here."

About five of the men raised their hands. One said, "I used to cut trees for a living if that's what you want to know."

Nomi said, "That's what I need to know as we are about to figure out how to cut all of the trees on the cliffside of this city."

Another man replied, "That might be a bit of a challenge, but I am sure we can figure out how to do it."

I asked, "What will we need?"

"The first thing," one of the other men said, "We should start at the bottom and work our way up."

I said, "That is kind of what we thought because if we cut from the top down, we would have a mess of cut trees to deal with, and someone might get killed."

"We have enough rope to start. We all take a line and climb up through the trees, then tie off one of them about fifty feet up. If we start cutting the trees on the bottom, we can move all of them away then climb up to the next ones, and so on," he explained.

"Boy, it's going to take some time just to get down there before we can even start cutting," one of the men responded.

Steve replied, "We can take care of that by finding what's down there and then opening a doorway."

"I will help if I can," one of the men from our base camp yelled.

"Me too," came the voices of a few others.

"The first thing we need is for you men who wish to start at the bottom of the cliffs to gather the equipment you will need. In the morning, somehow, Steve and I will find out where we need to create an opening," I reported.

Nomi said, "We will need people up here to help clear good paths in different directions to trees we need to cut down as well."

Several other people were saying they were not tree cutters but would do what they could to help cut down the ones up here.

Chapter 21

Water, Wind, and Exploring

Morning came, and we seemed to have less fog than we had in days past. As Bailey and I got out of the wagon, Steve raised his head, looked over at me, then said, "I will take care of this."

The next thing I knew, a massive blast of wind was blowing all around the entire top of the mountain. I looked over at him and said, "Thank you."

All of us wandered over to what I guess one might call a cafeteria, as it's where everyone cooked and ate their meals. One of the soldiers from Mortice's group walked up and spoke to Magness and Staggerus, asking them, "Is it possible to create a hot-water tank out of the metal that is in different places of the city?"

Staggerus replied, "I am sure we can do that. Does anyone have an idea where we will build it?"

"Carter, how did you have hot water around here long ago?" Magness asked.

"Oh, I guess I should have pointed that out to you before, but my mind is still trying to catch up. Do you see that large building in the center over there?" she asked as she pointed to a building that looked to be in the center of town. She continued, "It's the big building near that smaller building, where we found the water valve."

Everyone with us turned and looked at the building she had pointed to, and Jack, who had been standing there, asked, "I see it. Does that have something to do with heating the water here?"

"Yes," she replied. "If you can get into that building, you will see huge places used to burn fires. Above those are the water pipes for the hot water."

Staggerus spoke out and said, "Maybe that would be a good thing to check out after we eat."

The soldier who spoke about a hot-water tank agreed. Soon, everyone was chatting away. Steve, Jack Burdock, and I discussed how to blow the trees on the side of the mountain, down the hill. Burdock said, "I guess we need to find out where we can see the east side of the mountain."

Masher, Agatha, and Sophia were discussing the idea of searching out those upper walkways after eating. Heather and Krystle and their pets joined in the discussion, with Krystle saying, "There are a lot of ways to get up to that, and I understand there are many ways that come down and enter other buildings."

Steve asked Carter, "How can we get a good view of the cliff area on the east side?"

She replied, "I'm not sure we can get over to that area because of all the growth I see in that direction."

"We will get to it if there is a place where we can view all of that," Steve said.

Most of the women were sitting there listening to all the conversations. Finally, Majjeem said, "I think it would be nice to have hot water around here."

Carter said, "Oh, I agree because I could use a good hot bath." Then she raised her arms and wiggled around and continued to say, "Can't you tell I have not had a good one for hundreds of years." Then everyone started laughing.

Bailey spoke up, asking, "Can't we eat breakfast first before we get started on everything else?"

Soon breakfast was over, and some of the people were setting out to light a few bonfires to keep the fog away and burn off some of the dried branches and brush. Our mothers, Carter, and Majjeem, all sat with Manna and talked about what might lie ahead of us. Catrina said, "I have seen a few things that might take place here. I have also seen a few things I believe take place near that city of the giants."

Carter asked, "What have you seen here?"

"I did see eyes in the wall of a cave or tunnel, and that turned out to be you. I can only tell you one other thing about my three visions at this time. I will wait and be sure the last thing happens before I speak of it. I had a view almost a year ago, of looking down a hill and seeing lots of trees all piled up someplace. Now I wonder if that might be here."

A few of the men who said they could cut up trees caught Steve and me as we were trying to scope out the eastern side of the town. They decided to join us, along with Dohadie and Datilina, as we walked in that direction. As we were heading northeast, our blacksmiths were working with Nomi and Burdock, with a group of others trying to clear a path to the big building Carter had talked about for the hot water.

"How high can you lift me?" Steve asked.

"Is this like a competition?" I asked.

He started laughing and then said, "If you lift me as high as you can, or at least as high as I need to be, that will allow me to look around."

"We can do that, or we could ask Max to join us. Then he can fly around and tell us what he sees. However, let's see if we can find a location worthwhile to start from," I replied.

One of the men with us said, "This looks like a deer path, and it might be a good way to go."

We looked at it and found it to be a helpful travel route, so we followed it. It took us close to the east wall, where it looked like they had jumped up and over the wall. We could look over the side there and see more trails coming up the hill that the deer must have used to get in here.

We turned back to the path as it continued north, but then after a few hundred feet, it started to turn back to town. We found an excellent wide area that looked like a place deer had bedded down at one time, and I asked Steve, "Are you ready?"

"As ready as I will ever be," he replied.

With my power I raised him into the air, he yelled down to me, "Hey, there is Sky and Jasmin."

"Well, don't forget to wave," I said.

Sky sent a thought asking, *Can Steve fly now as well as yell?*

Oh, no, we are trying to find out what all the sides of this cliff area look like, I replied.

Oh, I see. Jasmin saw him and asked me if he could fly now, so I thought I would check and see. Where you are is difficult to see you, as most of what we can see around that location is brush and trees.

I kind of figured that. We are having a hard time clearing some of these places.

If you need it, we can come back over that area like we did that last time and burn off some of that brush, and overgrowth if you like.

Well, let us find out what is here first.

That's fine, I guess Jasmin is flying around Steve now as she can see him over all that greenery.

I see that.

You get back to what you need to do. Jasmin and I will be near by.

Stay safe, Sky, I said.

Steve sent a thought saying, *I see where we could be standing and use our powers to clear off some of the trees on the side of this mountain.*

Can we get to it?

Yes, it's just north of where you are now. Bring me down, and I will show you how we get there.

As he landed on the ground again, he said, "We have to go this way." And he started walking with the rest of us following. As we cut our way through a crowded area of brush, it wasn't long before we found what looked like a large stage of some kind almost hidden by greenery.

As we got closer, we were still working on getting past all the overgrowth. However, now we could see what looked like a viewpoint.

It was a platform that looked as if it had been carved out of the mountain. Near the cliffside was a small wall. We climbed up on the platform, then reached out to see if the wall was sturdy. Finding it to be solid, we leaned against it, seeing how thick all the trees had grown over the years.

Steve said, "Let's just get rid of all this brush and stuff now. What do you say?"

Where we were now standing still had lots of brush, vines, and different kinds of thistles.

I said, "If we can remove all of that from this viewpoint, let's do it without taking out that wall next to us."

We could see the cliff and all the trees close to where we were standing, on the other side of a four-foot-high wall. So we moved back to the end of the platform, and both of us produced enough power and blast to remove all the debris. I produced the power to move all the brush, branches, and vines, then Steve blew them away.

We stepped over to the center of the platform, and now we had a safe place to stand. As the others joined us, we started looking over the side of the cliff. Steve looked at me, and he asked, "You're not going to yell kerplop, are you, buddy?"

After I stopped laughing, I said, "This view does not bother me yet, like that back at Etheral. Here I see a lot of trees."

He replied, "You do understand that once we start blowing all of these trees down the hill, there will be one huge drop-off here that is probably going to be worse than what we had back there."

"That is true, but we still have a wall in front of us. However, I may still yell kerplop when all the trees are gone," I replied.

"Can we do this to the bottom of the hill?" Steve asked.

"I don't know. I do know one thing and that is, I want to be secure up here, and you will need to be secured as well," I replied.

"Dohadie, I'm going to have someone bring out some rope. Will you please keep an eye open for them?" I asked.

"Yes, but how . . . Oh, never mind, I know how you're going to contact them," he commented.

After reaching out to Bailey, I asked her, *Would you please have Nomi or a few of his men join us at the wall with a couple of good long ropes? Oh, and ask Max to join us as well.*

She was looking all around and asked me, *What wall?*

I turned to Steve and said, "She can't see us, so I'm going to raise you into the air, and you can wave at her as you did with Jasmin."

I used my power to raise him in the air, and as I was doing that, he looked like he was having a hard time staying in the same position. Steve soon gained his balance and was waving away.

I contacted Bailey again with Steve in the air, asking, *Can you see Steve?*

Oh my gosh, has he learned how to fly? she asked.

No, I raised him off the ground so you and Nomi could see where we are, I stated.

Staggerus, Magness, Burdock, and Nomi had reached the building that Carter had spoken about, and they were about to try to open the double doors.

Bailey had been speaking to Vanessa as I sent her my thoughts. After replying she noticed Max nearby and asked, "Max, can you go over to where you see Steve in the air and help them?"

He looked around for a few minutes. Suddenly he tipped his head a bit, looking this way and that as he viewed Steve in the air. Max started shaking his head, then said, "Sure."

Bailey then asked Vanessa and the pets with them to join her, and they walked over to the building where Nomi and the blacksmiths were.

As they walked up Bailey stated, "Nomi, Marty just contacted me asking me to see if you and a few of your men could please bring them a couple of ropes."

He replied, "I thought they were searching for the side of the mountain."

She said, "That is what they were doing, and if you look up in the sky, you can see where they are now."

All the other men heard Bailey say that and were now searching the sky, looking to see what she was talking about. Seeing Steve, they were tipping their heads this way and that to check to find a pole or something he was standing on. But all they viewed was space between his feet and the greenery far below.

Nomi also started looking, then suddenly noticed Steve up in the air above all the buildings, trees, and brush. "How is he up in the sky like that?"

"I think Marty lifted him up there so you and a few of your men would know where they are as they need a couple of good lengths of rope. We will stay here and do what we can to help until you get back," she stated.

"Very well, I will leave a few men with you and get him that rope," he replied.

As he ran off to get the rope, he and one of his men with him kept looking back at Steve floating in the air.

Soon, Max showed up and a few minutes later Nomi and his men showed up, then it was time to put that rope to use. "Max, we may need your flying skills soon," Steve said.

"Dohadie, would you please tie us off? We don't want to blow ourselves into space."

As they looked over the edge, Nomi asked, "Do you think you two can create a huge wind and power to clear off the entire side of this mountain?"

I stated, "This area has fewer trees and may be the best section of those trees to blow down the hill."

"Marty and I have talked about the kind of trees we see and back home pine trees like this can be blown over in a good windstorm," Steve replied.

Datilina asked, "How can you tell what is down there even though they are all spread out?"

"Well, that's where Max comes in because we are just going by what Carter said. As she told us it's a sheer cliff, and over the years, the trees started growing, and that's how people got in here to try to kill those who used to live here."

Dohadie asked, "Well, it's true there is not a lot here compared to other places we can see, but that is still a large number of trees to blow down the hill?"

I replied, "We understand that, but what we have to do is try and if we can't get them all down the hill, Steve and I may have to go down there and climb up and finish the job."

As Dohadie and the others were securing us by tying us to massive trees located behind the platform. I said to Max, "We need you to flap your wings and let us know if there is anything down below us, we could damage."

Soon, Max was changing, and everyone around was just standing there watching as he turned into a small bird. Some of those who had never seen him do that when we first visited Etheral were watching him and they were weaving back and forth, watching him change as if they had been out partying all night and could not believe what was happening.

Soon, Max was in the air flying all around and growing in size. He was having a good time, it seemed, flying over all those trees, up and down and across the side of this mountain. *Marty, there are no buildings or things like that, only trees,* he said.

Alright, Max, what do you think? Can we blow those trees down the hill? I asked.

He replied, *I have seen you and Steve do some amazing things, but even though this is not the largest number of trees, you said a lot of dirt will be packed around those roots. So, I don't know. However, I know both of you have enough power, force, and wind to get most of them out of the ground.*

Thank you, come on back here so you're safe, I said.

On my way, he replied, and soon a large bird flying over us turned into a smaller bird, then landed near all of us. Suddenly there was Max again.

"What do you think, Max?" I asked.

"I don't know, Marty. There are places where there are fewer trees but still a lot of trees, and you told me lots of dirt as well will be holding them in the ground."

I stood there looking toward the ground, thinking for a moment, then looked at Steve, asking him, "I know my powers have been growing and I can feel yours have as well, but if we start pushing these to the bottom, we won't be able to stop."

"That is true, so both of us better make sure we do it completely. If we don't, you and I will be heading down this hill to do it again, which to me does not sound good, and I know you sure won't like that idea at all," he replied.

"You are correct, we will have to build up our power, and if we need to, we hit it with a second burst," I replied.

"Max, so there were smaller trees down there?" Steve asked.

"Most of the trees were not that large, and they seemed to be spread out. From my point of view, I think the two of you should do what you can. I feel the two of you will take care of most of those trees if not all of them," Max replied.

CHAPTER 22

Water House

Back at that building that Nomi just left, they still had their share of problems. Most of what had been in front of those doors had been removed. They hoped those doors would now open freely, but our metalsmiths and a few other people pulled on the barn door gate handles, and nothing happened. Those handles alone were fourteen-inch-tall cast iron. And this place had two doors.

Again, two men on each door handle and nothing was happening.

Bailey said, "Tabby, please step back a bit and wait here." Bailey and Vanessa walked over, with Vanessa asking, "Why not let us give it a try?"

Both of them grabbed a handle, pulling as hard as they felt they could. Nothing happened. Bailey and Vanessa both looked at each other as the men around them were shaking their heads and had huge smiles on their faces. Vanessa asked, "We can do what the guys can do, right?"

The two of them each grabbed a door handle again and pulled with nothing happening. Finally, they looked around at the guys near them, who were all giving off the feelings of "Okay, girls." Then both stepped back a few feet, looked at those doors, then at each other, shook their heads, and Bailey asked, "We can do this, right?"

Vanessa nodded her head and said, "Girl, we can do anything." Then both started laughing. Soon everyone who was around them joined in.

Walking up to those doors, each one of them grabbed a handle on a door. As they pulled, both doors creaked and vibrated. They kept pulling and those doors began to move. Slowly at first, very slowly, but they were both determined. The dirt around the bottom of those doors was slowly moving. Both doors were shaking. Suddenly both doors swung open, crushing any remaining brush and vines and smashing small trees as they were slammed back against the building. All the people around them were having a flash of what had become an unexpected and unbelievable moment.

"Wow!" seemed to be the loudest word coming out of the mouths of those around them at first. Then everyone around the two of them was shaking their heads and saying that was awesome, fantastic, and unbelievable.

One of the guys spoke out and said, "I knew you two could do great things, but you just showed all of us who the bosses really are." Then everyone laughed.

As they entered the building, they found that most of the interior was not bad for a building this old. "We could use a few torches in here," Staggerus said.

Soon, with better light, they noticed many things, like pipes running all over the place with valves and stairs leading down to a lower level. "I guess we need to go down there," Magness said as he pointed to the broad set of stone steps leading down.

Everyone tried to gather around those with the light as they wanted to see all that was there. Finally, one of the men in the group said, "I'm going to run back and grab a few more torches. Does anyone else want anything?"

"Please grab me one of those torches," one of the crew yelled. Soon others were saying, "One for me too, please," as hands shot up in the air. He took a count and ran off. One or two of the others waited by the doorways for him to return, and the rest walked on to explore more of what was down below.

Staggerus said, "Look at the size of those burn boxes. They are large enough to heat all the water for the entire town."

Bailey said, "Well, I guess that takes care of our hot-water problem if it still works."

Magness asked, "Look up above them. Do you think those are large sliding doors to allow heat to rise out of the building when they are using those?"

His brother commented, "That is probably exactly what they are for."

Someone else asked, "What is this for?"

As the group walked over to see what he found, they noticed a large round lid that looked like a cap of some kind. Two of the men attempted to pry it up and then lift it open. Suddenly all turned to look at Vanessa and Bailey. Bailey and Vanessa looked at each other, and Bailey said, "Not sure, but I feel we started something."

As Vanessa nodded, both of them walked over, and as one of the men placed a pry bar under the edge, he lifted it about an inch. Another man placed a chunk of wood in there, and they pried it a bit more. It was just enough for Vanessa and Bailey to do the rest.

As the two of them lifted that huge cover, they turned it to the side, and it rolled for a few feet and finally landed on the ground. There was a massive hole with a ladder in it.

Bailey and Vanessa both looked down inside, and they leaned over and tried to see what was down there. Suddenly both of them leaned back, and looked at each other, with Bailey saying, "Nope, not me. I'm not going down inside that thing."

Vanessa said, "Hey, what she said works for me as well. I'm not stepping into that hole."

A few others who had waited for torches now had them and walked down the stairs, looking all around. Some of them noticed the furnaces and one of them said, "I have never seen any burn boxes this size before."

All of them gathered around and looked at them, then turned to see others about ready to climb into a hole.

"We have a few more torches here," one of the men yelled.

"That's good," Magness said.

"Let's see what we have down there," Nomi's right-hand man, John, said. Then he grabbed a torch and started down the ladder. When he reached the bottom, he yelled up, "I need a few hands down here, and you will need more light."

Soon men were climbing down into the hole. When they reached the bottom, they found what looked like tunnels going in all directions.

John said, "I guess we should find what is going where and why."

"Well, let's break off into teams of three. We will walk down one tunnel, come back, then we can check out any others," Staggerus said.

As everyone grabbed partners and started walking off, Bailey, Vanessa, Ziggy, Agatha, and Tabby were still upstairs looking around. The building was large and accommodated the two large furnaces. As they walked into other sections of the building, they found a hall that must have been designed to be away from any heat, and it had several rooms. One looked to be a supply room; another must have been a storage room. At the end of that hall was another closed door. As they opened it, they found papers, charts, and maps on a huge table. They also noticed places on the walls with rolls of paper in them. The ones on the table in front of them seemed very fragile. "I'm not sure we should try to move these," Bailey said.

Vanessa said, "I agree, as they look like they could fall apart, and it seems these are maps for what they are looking at down below."

Tabby spoke out, saying, "What we need to do is find someone who can draw and ask them to reproduce the pages before they are removed."

Bailey said, "I'm going to speak to John. I will be right back." Then she walked away and headed to the hole in the ground.

She stood there and yelled down, "John, can you hear me?"

A faint voice was heard saying, "Just a minute, and I will walk back."

As he showed up a few minutes later, he asked, "I'm here. What do you need?"

"There is a room up here that we need to keep everyone out of until we can find someone to reproduce what we think are maps. Can you please look but make sure no one touches them as they might fall apart?" Bailey asked.

"Just a minute and I will join you and look." Then he yelled at the other men saying, "I will be going back up above, so carry on." Soon he was standing next to Vanessa, Bailey, Tabby, Agatha, and Ziggy at a huge table.

As all of them turned and looked all around the room, they viewed rolls of paper stuffed into shelves along the walls, and the table in front of them looked like it was the layout of this entire city water system.

John walked around the room, looking at all the tables and everything in cubbyholes then looked at the girls, saying, "I think this room holds all the information regarding every tunnel and location for the water that comes from down below."

"What do you think?" Vanessa asked.

"I think we need to make sure no one comes in here until we copy everything in this room," he replied.

"What do you want to do to protect them?" Ziggy asked.

"I can place a few people here to make sure no one enters this room," he replied.

Ziggy, Agatha, and Tabby looked at each other, then Agatha spoke out, saying, "While someone finds a person or people who can make drawings of these, we can wait here as long as it takes because this seems very important."

Bailey said, "That's a good idea, you three make sure no one enters this room, and I will go find one or two people who can read and copy all this information."

Bailey found a few from Anthony's group and asked, "Can any of you copy maps or draw?"

"I know someone who used to draw maps back home. Why do you ask?" one of the women inquired.

"If she is here, we need her help to copy very old papers before they get destroyed," Bailey replied.

The woman stood up, looked in one direction, turned, and looked back the other way, then suddenly rotated her head back as if she noticed something and leaned one way then the other as if searching and straining her vision to view someone. All at once she was waving her arms around and yelled, "Glomera, can you please come over here?"

Soon a young woman who looked to be Asian was running over and finally stood with Bailey and the woman who called her. "What can I do for you, Egana?" she asked.

"Glomera, this is Bailey, and she has a problem I feel you may be able to solve," Egana stated.

As the three of them spoke, Bailey soon learned about this young lady, and all three of them were soon walking back to the water building.

Once inside, they were greeted by Ziggy, Tabby, and Agatha.

Looking at all the papers, Glomera said, "I can copy these, but they will all need to be moved slowly and gently, one at a time."

Egana spoke up, saying, "I can help and one other person that might be of help would be that other woman you used to work with when you made those maps."

Glomera replied, "She is here, but I am not sure where."

Bailey asked, "What do we need to copy all these papers?"

"Oh, we need paper—lots of paper—and measuring tools and writing tools, and we must have all that set up before we even begin. We need to make sure no one enters this room until we begin and then only us because the smallest amount of movement will destroy many of these pages. So I think we need to return to Etheral and get as many clean large sheets of paper as we can find," Glomera stated.

As the women were discussing one problem, others were taking care of another.

"Alright, are you really ready to do this?" I asked.

Steve looked at me, then looked back over the side of the hill and said, "I think we can do this, Marty."

I turned and looked at those with us and said, "Please be sure our powers don't push us into space."

The men with us all laughed, and one of them said, "Marty, if you go into the air, that wall, those trees, and all of us go too."

"Let's do it," I said.

"Hold on a minute," Steve said.

"What is it?" I asked.

"Well, I just thought if we can't clear off the entire side of this mountain, you and I will have to go down to where we clear it and do this all over again."

"Steve, we already discussed this," I replied.

"Sorry, I bought that up again," he said.

"I have a question for you. If we grow in height so we are bigger, will that give us more power?" I asked.

"Wow. Now that's a weird one. So you think if we grow, the powers we have may grow?"

"I don't know. I was just wondering," I replied.

As Steve was pointing to the trees below, he asked, "How about if we try to clear this smaller section, and if that works, we try farther over that way at another time?"

A voice spoke up, asking, "Are you two going to do this or not?" It was Dohadie.

Both Steve and I turned at the same time, and both of us said, "Yes."

Then we turned around. I said, "We will find out about that height thing another time. Let's get this done."

Suddenly the sound of winds like that of a tornado, along with an explosion, took place.

All three of the women and the pets ran outside the water building to see what happened. Looking all around, they saw nothing that could have been an explosion, so Bailey said, "One of you please stay here with Ziggy, Tabby, and Agatha. Whoever looks for that other person can see if you can find her and some of the tools you need as well. I will find someone to open a door so you can get all that paper."

Glomera stated, "I will stay here with them and make sure no one touches any of these papers until you both return."

"That would be good. John may come up to check on this room, as he already viewed all of this, and we agreed to find someone who can read and copy everything here. It looks like these are drawings of all the pipes, lines, tunnels, and places water goes to," Bailey said.

Agatha commented, "If he comes back, we will explain we have found maybe three people to copy everything here, but it will take time. I will tell him we are going to stay here until you return with the other people and the paper you need for copying everything."

"That will be good, all of you stay here and we will return as soon as we can," Bailey said.

Egana and Bailey both ran toward the wagons, and Bailey noticed others running in the direction where she had seen Steve floating in the air. "Please see if you can find that other woman. I am going to see what happened and find a few who are heading back to Etheral. I will meet you over by the wagons in the center of town," Bailey said.

Egana replied, "I will try to find her and, see you soon."

CHAPTER 23

Remarkable Powers

I was building up my power. Steve was taking massive breaths of air as if to enlarge his lungs. I looked over at him and he gave me the thumbs up, then both of us let it rip. Winds began to howl and blow. My power burst out like a massive attack on the forest below. Trees were bending, twisting, and being ripped from the ground with tons of dirt on their roots, and with Steve's wind, they were propelled down the mountainside. Soon, Steve took another deep breath and blasted away again. We were both using powers we had not used before. Soon we were looking at the terrain at the base of the hill, with vast stacks of trees, branches, and tons of dirt piled high upon one another.

I suddenly got light-headed, and my legs felt like rubber, and Steve reached out and grabbed me, pulling me away from the wall in front of us. We looked at each other and nodded.

Then Dohadie and the men with us walked up and looked over the edge, saying, "Oh my lords," "Totally unreal," and "I can't believe all those trees are now on the ground at the bottom of this hill."

People were coming our way, yelling and screaming, "What's going on?" "What was that noise?" Soon there were many other questions relating to an explosion and massive winds.

Art and Tom ran up, with Art asking, "What the heck is going on? Has this place been attacked?"

Tom asked, "Did the two of you create all that noise?"

"Well, if you look over the wall, you will now see all those trees are at the bottom of the hill," Steve replied.

They climbed up on the platform and looked over the side. Tom said, "Marty, you got most of them but not all of them. Look at that patch of trees over there." As he pointed to the one place Steve had pointed to earlier on the other side of that wall, I looked at him, stayed where I was standing, and just nodded my head.

Steve said, "Marty does not like heights. It's kind of like me as I don't like snakes. So you won't get him over there again now that we can see the base of this mountain."

"Well, many people don't like heights, so it's kind of a natural reaction. There are many things I don't like," Art said.

Tom spoke, saying, "I have never had a fear of heights, but there are many other things that can disturb my day."

Nomi said, "I have a few things that I dislike, but that's why I spend so much time out here in this region."

"What is that, Nomi?" Art asked.

"Mostly my in-laws. I miss my kids and wife, but not them," he replied.

Everyone around us started laughing.

Bailey, Carter, and our mothers were soon joining us. Carter asked, "Was that you two that made all that noise?"

Steve looked over at Carter and said, "Yes, we did. If you look over the side, you will now see most of those trees are gone."

Masher, Heather, and Krystle, along with their protectors, stopped walking around that walkway over the edge of the town, and Heather sent a thought asking, *Did you just blow something up?*

Well, I guess you could say we did as we just cleared off the side of the cliff area. We blew all the trees down to the bottom of the mountain.

Will that make it simpler for people to cut them up?

I hope so. Where are you?

Masher, my sister, our pets, and I are walking around this walkway. Whatever you did reverberated throughout this entire place.

You stay safe.

We will.

Tasha, Meesha, and Majjeem came up, with Majjeem asking, "Did you create all that noise?"

Dohadie asked, "They did get a bit noisy, didn't they?"

Anthony, his men, and more of Nomi's men walked up, looking at everyone, and noticed many looking over the wall. Soon everyone was now walking over to the wall, viewing what looked like many hundreds of trees in a pile. The dust and dirt were still floating around. Anthony said, "I gather it was you two that created that explosion."

"I'm afraid it was louder than we thought it would be," I replied.

Nomi stated, "I think none of us expected these two to make such a load noise."

More people were now arriving and looking all around, viewing others looking over the wall, so they made a line, and everyone took their turn checking out the view. They soon noticed all the trees were now at the base of the hill. Our mothers turned and walked back over to where we were standing, and Catrina spoke out, saying, "I just looked over the wall and saw the vision I had almost a year ago and never understood why I was looking down the hill at all kinds of trees in large piles like that."

"That's all you saw," Bailey asked.

Catrina shrugged her shoulders, squeezed her lips together, tipped her head, and stood there with a lack-of-information look on her face, saying, "It's all I saw, and it was just weird until just a few minutes ago."

Carter walked over and asked, "The two of you pushed all those trees down that hill?"

"Well, I am not sure you could say, 'pushed them down the hill' because we didn't use our hands and push anything. But we managed to blow them down there with our power and lots of wind," Steve replied.

Vanessa said, "We found out where the hot water is created, and as we walked out of that building, we heard you two do your thing. It sounded like more of an explosion than just wind from Steve."

"Well, I built up my power to add with it, and by the time we were done, we had created more force than both of us have created before," I said.

Vanessa, standing there grinning ear to ear reminded me of a little girl who was so proud of what she accomplished, suddenly asked in that happy little-girl voice, "Well, guess what?"

Steve turned and noticed her look of excitement and the way she just spoke, then tipped his head and then, with a "What's that all about?" look, asked, "What?"

"Bailey and I did something Magness and Staggerus could not do even with the help of Nomi's men," she said.

I asked, "What was that?"

Vanessa said, "Well, they could not open the doors to that building we found, and they tried to pull them open with all of them together. Bailey and I were standing there watching, and after they tried a few times, the two of us asked, 'What if we try?'"

Bailey continued, "We got some funny looks from the guys, but we walked over and pulled on those doors. It took us a few times and finally they began to move, and when they finally opened, it was with such force they swung out, crushing bushes and vines and even a few small trees as they slammed back against the building."

Vanessa added, "Yes, it was not easy at first, but by the time we took the third shot, we figured it was time to make it happen, and we did it."

John said, "On top of that, when we got inside, none of us could remove a huge cover on a hole in the ground, and after two of our men pried it up a bit, it was too heavy to lift. These two walked up and lifted it off. So I think you two young men are in for some competition."

All of us stood there, amazed. Tom and Art had been listening, and they both looked at each other, with Art saying to the girls, "I guess we missed all the action."

Tom replied, "I guess we did."

Vanessa replied, "You did."

"So tell me, when are you planning on more muscular feats and explosions so we can watch?" Art asked.

"So you're saying we could actually see lots more explosions from all four of them?" one of the men standing near asked.

Everyone started to laugh.

"We need to open a doorway to that area down there. We must move some of those trees so people can work on them to remove those roots, branches, and limbs," I disclosed.

Wanda said, "It looks like you need to have a good flash flood or a rainstorm to get all the dirt off the roots of those trees."

Nomi and Anthony were both talking, and Nomi asked, "After we view that area down there, we will need to return to Etheral and get more people."

"I think that it might be a good idea. If we can get all those trees trimmed up and ready for the mill, we can open another door to the mill and get them all cut," I replied.

Suddenly, Bailey spoke out, saying, "We found what look like drawings and plans to all the water pipe routes and tunnels, but we must have a couple of people copy them and not destroy the old plans that are there. All the plans and papers cannot be moved without a gentle touch, and now we need to return to Etheral and get lots of large sheets of paper and pencils."

"Well, I guess we get more help and you can get whatever it is you need to copy the drawings. So, who is going with you, and who is keeping those plans safe?" I asked.

"One other woman from Anthony's group will go with me to get lots of paper. Tabby, Ziggy, and Agatha with another woman from Anthony's group are waiting for us," she replied.

"Sounds like you will need a few others with you for help, and may need a large wagon?" I commented.

"We will need a wagon if we get as much paper as we saw over there," she replied.

"Okay, everyone, let's head back to the center of town," Steve yelled.

Soon, Bailey and Egana and a few others were hitching up horses to a wagon and riding through a door into upper Etheral. "Egana, you probably know where we need to go, so we will follow you," Bailey stated.

After finding a location with lots of paper, they loaded the wagon and opened another door to return. Several people were there when they returned, to give them all a hand with taking a good amount of that paper to the water house.

Marty, Steve, Tom, Art, and the girls all had their arms loaded with stacks of paper and, as they entered that room, the pets and Glomera were surprised to see all the people loaded down with paper and pencils and other measuring utensils. "My gosh," Glomera said. "You did it. Please place all that paper on the table over in the corner and the other things in that big box next to it, and we will get to work."

The desk was so large that they could bring papers over and lay them out next to the ones they wished to copy, and after looking at everything, Glomera stated, "Oh, this will be so much fun, but we all must be very careful."

Everyone was looking at the papers and Tom said, "All of us need to get out of this room, except those who will be copying everything."

As all of them were walking out of the door, Bailey said, "I agree, so let's get Steve out of here before he takes another deep breath."

Then everyone turned and looked at Steve as he was shaking his head and dropping it to his chest. Then he lifted his head and replied, "I think Marty and I used most of our powers on those trees."

Walking back to the center of town, they were all talking about how those papers looked like they could not be moved without damaging them.

Art said, "We are very lucky to even have found them in that good of condition. I guess the weather and elements never got to them."

Steve commented, "Finding all the plans for that water system will be one great find if all those papers can be copied."

Everyone agreed with that.

CHAPTER 24

The Return

Walking back, all of us gathered in the park area, and were discussing what we would be doing next. Nomi was saying, "Now that we have plans for all the water lines in this city, that should really help find locations we can use to fill our water containers rather than going to that well."

"I agree, but we still may need to travel and fill our water tanks again," I added.

As Bailey asked me a question, she was standing there waiting for my reply, but suddenly, I had a conversation in my head, so I raised my hand and held up one finger, tapping my head to let her know someone just contacted me.

Marty, why don't you find that one woman who was in love and return to that rock slab?

Anubis, is that you?

You already know it is. Then I thought I heard a laugh.

OK, let me round her up. We will be over there shortly.

"Sorry, Bailey, was not trying to be rude, but someone called. Carter, would you please come with me? We need to return to that rock slab where we found Zane's bones," I said.

Our mothers, Bailey, Majjeem, and everyone else turned as I spoke those words. Then I shook my head as if to say yes. It looked like a small parade as all of us walked back to the location where we found his bones. Walking over to that location, I said, "We need to make sure we wait back here," as I wanted to make sure Anubis had room for him to arrive.

We are here, I mentally said.

The ground began to shake as it seemed to separate in front of us. Dirt and dust flew all around him. A mist rose from the ground, and suddenly Anubis was rising in front of everyone in a cloud of that dust.

I could feel all the different ways people were thinking of how he came to us and how some feared him while others found him interesting, and everyone was looking as he rose from the ground and stood in front of us. Carter asked the question, all of us had in our minds, "Did he bring him back?"

"We will soon see," I said.

You must keep in mind the size of Anubis, a very big figure as well as very tall. We waited as the dust cleared, then we heard him speak, saying, "He is here."

All of us were looking for an additional person. Suddenly someone walked out from behind Anubis. It was a young man that looked about the same age as Carter. Carter suddenly noticed Zane and ran up to him with tears in her eyes. She wrapped her arms around him and started crying and saying, "I have missed you so much."

As everyone ran past Anubis, he walked back to where I was standing off to the side of everyone else. It looked like the entire camp was gathering around Zane and Carter. All I could feel at this time was love from everyone.

"Hey, buddy," Anubis said.

I walked up to him and rose to meet his height. I reached out my hand and arm. Both of us grasped each other's forearms, and I said, "Thank you so much, my friend. I now owe you."

"Oh no, you don't owe me anything, Marty. It's I that still owe you. If it were not for you and those with you, I would still be a slave myself."

"Well, thank you. Is Zane going to be everything he once was?" I asked.

"He will be as he was before he died," he replied.

As we talked, I looked over and noticed Carter introducing Zane to everyone around them. Everyone was excited to see him alive again. I still felt love, excitement, and happiness. I turned to my friend and said, "You have made two people very happy, and I am sure their love will continue to grow."

"I feel you are right, my friend. However, I must say goodbye, for now."

We looked at each other and I asked, "Are you telling me you're busy?"

"But of course, my friend, but you know how to reach me if you need my help," he replied.

I replied, "Again, thank you, buddy." Then both of us nodded our heads, grasped each other's forearms, and laughed one more time.

As he stepped back to give us distance, A cloud of dirt and dust was created, the ground shook, opened, and a large mist rose from that opening, then Anubis was gone. Suddenly everyone turned toward me as I was still about ten feet in height. As Carter and Zane were talking, he looked over at me and yelled, "Marty!"

As I was shrinking back to my regular self, he was walking up to me and tossed his arms around me, saying, "I don't know how any of this is possible, but thank you, dear friend."

I looked at him in a manner that I am sure showed all kinds of questions. Finally, I said, "You must be Zane."

"Yes, I am, but you already know that. If it were not for you coming to us before those people attacked, surely all of those in this town would have died. So, thank you again for saving everyone."

"Zane, I am sorry, but you have me mixed up with someone else. Maybe just returning and seeing me at the height made you think I was another person. But I must assure you, I'm not."

"Marty, how would I even know your name if we had not met before?" he asked.

I replied, "I am sure Carter, or someone must have mentioned my name to you while you were meeting everyone."

In a quiet voice he commented, "If you say so, I understand. I am sure you don't want everyone else to know," he said.

Bailey asked me, "Marty, could it have been some past relative named Marty?"

"I'm not sure, but I guess anything is possible," I replied.

I looked at all the people standing there with questioning thoughts and feelings of wondering and said, "Well, I think we have a great reason for a celebration."

Carter ran up and gave me a great big hug and a kiss, saying, "Thank you for bringing the one person I love back to me."

"You're very welcome, and I would do it again just to feel all that happiness and love between you two."

All of us walked over to the area cleared out for our meals and sat around, talking. Finally, Medina walked over and sat down beside me, saying, "Marty, people with powers can move through time. Maybe you did go back in time and help them."

"I think I understand that . . ." I thought for a moment, then continued, "But it was not me as far as I can tell," I replied.

Zane stood up on a bench and said, "I am so happy to be alive again and with Carter one more time. "Marty, I understand you made that happen, so you can't deny that one."

I stood up and said, "I was not sure that could be done, but I had to try to reach out to a friend, and he made it happen."

"Thank you," he replied.

"You're very welcome. I am glad we got you back," I said.

Everyone was chatting away, and I looked over at Art. He was looking directly at me, so I tipped my head as if to give him a direction to the right. Both of us walked away from all the others and were soon meeting outside the building. He asked me, "Are you now wondering if it was you?"

"Yes, I am."

"Let's walk, and we can discuss this away from anyone else," he replied.

As we walked, he was telling me a story about how sometimes events take place that never should. "You see, Marty, when all of us arrived here, those gates were not closed. They stood wide open. We had to clear large areas of trees and brush, and we even found Carter in that room."

He looked at me and was now giving off a feeling of sadness, with an expression that was one of grief as he continued, "What we found was destruction as if hundreds of people entered this city. We viewed the skeletal remains of people everywhere we looked. Many men, women, and children had lost their lives, and when all of us viewed that, I felt sick and lost. I could tell you and everyone around me was feeling that same way."

I asked, "So, we came here two times?"

"No, after you found Carter and she regained all her feelings and memory, she told us how people came charging in the open gates as a few others were climbing the cliff area to attack and kill all people for whatever gold or silver they had. She told all of us that she and Zane did what they could. But it was negligible, as their spells could not stop them. The entire town was plundered by people who had come to this region to kill and steal from the giants. This town was one they found that seemed like a good target.

"Those who came did not consider that not only were there giants here, but Denarians, elves, and people of all kinds of races, sizes, and beliefs. All of those living here were happy working in friendship and building good lives. And all of those who entered this city wanted to destroy, steal, and kill for their individual gain."

"How can it be that no one remembers that?" I asked.

"It's as we changed events with that creature and his family. No one knew except you, Steve, and me," he replied.

"After viewing all the remains and destruction, you asked me, 'Why do all the good people have to die so the worst can live in wealth?'" Art commented.

I asked, "So did you send me back to stop it?"

"Both you and I went back, and it was you who talked to Zane. You warned him to close the gates and guard that wall on the cliffs until he and Carter could soon move all the people out of the town to safety. At first, he did not believe you, and I watched as you started to grow as you did here today. One of the things I believe that gave him faith in you was when you had grown in height and walked over, placing your hand on the wording of the rock, and it opened."

"Why would that make a difference?" I asked.

"Because they knew that could happen. However, it was always the townspeople that knew, not outsiders. They understood it led to an underground passageway to the east side of the mountain. No one had gone down there for many years. No one used that to get water as there was a valve in the building nearby to shut the water off, if need be," he replied.

"So because Carter had told us about how to get the water, I was the one that showed them how they needed to escape?"

"In a manner of speaking. You simply reminded Zane that route was there so people could get out safely," he declared.

"All this sounds so unreal. We walked up and found him and told him about what was to happen?" I asked.

"Yes, and the entire town was now warned ahead of time because of you."

"How come he never said he saw you?" I asked.

"To him, I was just a child and he had no idea I was anyone other than one of the town's children. You became your regular size again and explained to him all you knew about what was going to happen. He yelled out to the people to close both entrances and lock them, and sent others to the wall."

"Zane yelled at Carter to join him as he was moving people down the steps after you told him to save the people. Before Carter ran up, you spoke with Zane and told him, 'Be sure to show Carter how to open this stone, and if you find there is no escape, run to the tower.'"

"I will do that, my friend," he replied.

You said, 'I must leave,' and as he was turning toward Carter, you said goodbye, and you turned to see me, and we walked off and vanished."

"So when he turned back to me, we were gone?"

"Yes, we were gone. Then when we came back this last time, we viewed no death or skeletal remains. You saved an entire city."

"You mean we saved an entire city," I commented.

I felt pleased I could do that, but at the same moment, I was thinking of how time should remain constant and not be changed. I thought of Germany and the concentration camps and the wars over the years and thought about past events showing us what not to do in the future.

"Do you understand now what happened?" Art asked.

"I do, and I am glad we could save this city," I replied.

"We did not change a lot when it comes to the timeline. Today, we have two people with us from that time who were able to save the lives of many and those with us should never know the fact of it all."

"I understand," I replied.

Art said, "So let's go join in the celebration."

CHAPTER 25

Getting Help

Everyone was still talking and having conversations about how Zane returned. As Art and I walked in, I noticed a few people were looking at us as we entered. Steve walked up and asked, "Hey, guys, what's going on?"

I sent a thought to Steve: *We will discuss what I found out later.*

OK, as you say, he replied.

People started to gather around Tom, Art, Steve, and me. "How could you contract a person of the dead to bring Zane back?" someone asked.

I stood there thinking for a moment then looked out at all the people, and Zane was looking right at me as I said, "I have found I have been able to do amazing things. Sometimes it has been because of some other amazing people I know. It's not just my powers that make things happen."

As Zane was standing there and still looking at me, he nodded his head yes.

The rest of the day seemed to be a day of pleasant conversation with new ideas. However, we still had to do something with all those trees down the hill. Some of Nomi's group were gathering tools and sharing them with Anthony and his crew.

They had found a good wagon in that long building we opened that looked like it was designed to haul heavy loads. After checking it over and making sure the wood was still good, I got to thinking it must be made of something like the oak that we had back home.

People were making sure it was ready to carry trees to the mill. Mortice talked about using two of their horses, which were smaller but would not have an actual heavy load to pull for any great distance once we opened the entrance to the location we had viewed.

Bailey asked, "Do you know where to go to get to the bottom of the hill?"

"I have viewed it and feel I know exactly what I need to look for," I replied.

Some of us spoke about getting more help from Etheral, and Anthony said, "That would be an excellent idea."

Lunchtime came and went. Now that people were getting ready to work on those trees, Magness and his brother agreed to work with a few of Nomi's men on that hot-water system.

Anthony and Nomi were both ready to return to Etheral to get more people, and Zane and Carter wanted to know if they could travel with us. So, when the doorway opened, I looked at both of them and saw total wonderment on their faces with eyes wide and full of excitement. Then as all of us gathered near the entrance Vanessa opened, I asked Zane and Carter, "Care to join us on a new adventure?"

The feelings I got were those of incredible enthusiasm and instantaneous delight. Both looked at me, and Zane looked at the opening one more time and then said, "We are with you."

Soon, all those returning to Etheral were walking out into the area we had left a few times before. I said to those who came back for supplies, "If you need to go up the hill, stay with us. Everyone else who is locating people, horses, wagons, and supplies in Lower Etheral and Old Etheral, please go with Phil."

As I watched our newest friends looking all around and viewing the road up to the hill, they saw something they had never expected to see. Bailey was speaking to Medina and telling her more about what was around us. Steve was talking to Tom and Art, telling them about some of the things they had not seen here. All our protectors were in human form, with Masher a bit larger than Ziggy, Agatha, and Tabby. Max was a kid again and loved it.

I said to Zane, "It's because of these people we have traveled into the lands you once called home. The region you now live in is considered the Denarian lands. The giants moved to another location and farther into the mountains many years after a great war. I imagine that great war was with people like those who wanted to kill all your town's people."

"So the giants still live?" Zane asked.

"From all I have learned during the years of the war, wise ones traveled to the west to help the giants, and many giants moved to the mountains near the dragons and the wise ones. Many other giants, however, had been digging into the mountain, and it's been said they found a huge land between massive mountain ranges and lived there. And maybe we will find out for sure," I stated.

"It's good they still live as many of them were not different from us or anyone else, other than size," Carter stated.

"The Denarians came and started to build new lives. They are trying to create a memorial to all those who lived in these lands centuries ago. Maybe it would be a good thing for the king, queen, and the elders to have your input about that part of history." Jack spoke up.

Carter and Zane looked at each other, and then Carter spoke, asking, "There is a king and queen around here?"

"There is and I am sure they would love to know you and learn more about their lands," I replied.

Zane spoke out, saying, "That would be wonderful. It would be like us teaching others the history of the lands."

"It would be, indeed," Jack replied.

Steve said, "That would sure give more facts to what happened during those times."

Jack said, "I think that more about the events back then would be one thing I would love to learn about myself."

Bailey, what do you think of introducing our newest friends to the king and queen? I sent.

Do you mean Art, Majjeem, Medina, and Tom? she replied.

Yes, that is what I mean, along with Zane and Carter, I continued.

She replied, *I think it would be marvelous.*

I broke out laughing at Bailey's use of older words, and everyone looked at me as if I was losing it.

I said to all those with us, "Now all of us are going up that hill."

Carter said, "I hope we don't have to walk all that way as it looks like one long road."

Zane added, "I have to agree with Carter. It seems like a road that will take a long time to walk. Will we get to the top before it gets dark?"

Tom, Art, Medina, and Majjeem all looked up at the road, and Medina said, "I would think you have a better way to reach the top of that hill."

Carter said, "I sure hope so. Can we get a few raptors to ride?"

Everyone looked at Carter, and I asked, "Have you ever ridden on a raptor?"

"Only once, and they are fast, but the one I was on didn't seem to want to go where he was supposed to go," she answered.

Everyone started to laugh, and she gave them a funny look. But Bailey said, "Not a long walk, and I don't wish to even see any raptors."

"Steve, care to do the honors?" I asked.

As Steve opened the doorway, I sent a thought to Bailey asking, *Do you think they tamed things like raptors for travel and such?*

Not sure, Marty, but remember someone told us when we first got here that they used monsters for things like that and for moving huge rocks in those mountains, Bailey replied.

I think George told us that when we first arrived, I said.

As the doorway opened, we were sitting in front of the gates to the palace.

Zane, Carter, Art, Tom, and Medina all walked through with the rest of us, who had already seen it before. As they walked out of the opening, they viewed the palace gates, but as the doorway closed, all of them turned and observed the town of Upper Etheral, then looked at us and then back at the palace in front of them.

"This city is massive in size," Zane stated.

Carter said, "I have never seen anything like this before."

As the gate began to open behind us, we all turned to see guards walking out to greet us, saying, "We have sent word to the elders about your arrival."

Those who needed to round up crew members were now walking off to other parts of the town. The rest of us followed the guards. Walking into the courtyard, we noticed Averell and Gram. I walked up and said, "It's so good to see you both again." As I said that, I wrapped my arms around my grandmother and gave her a big hug.

Gram said, "Marty, I have missed you, but it seems you have done well."

Averell said, "What a pleasant surprise. It seems you have new members to your group."

"We do," I replied.

Bailey started introducing everyone, and soon Mincer and Tangent joined us. Everyone was talking about different things as Zane and Carter discussed how much they loved what they saw here. Others were talking about the new city on the hill we found. Majjeem and Medina were speaking to the elders about the towns of Etheral and all the people. Gram and I, along with Ziggy, walked a bit away so we could talk.

Soon several guards came toward us and so did Tom, Art, Medina, Majjeem, Carter, and Zane. All those with us gathered around me with Zane asking, "Have we done something wrong?"

Gram said, "No, no, not at all. If I am not mistaken, they are guarding the king and queen."

"The king and queen?" Carter asked.

"Yes, Carter, you're about to meet the king and queen of the Denarians," Steve said.

Soon all of us were greeting King Haskin and Queen Natalie as they walked up to us. Haskin was saying, "Marty, it's great to see all of you again. It seems you have a few more with you today."

"Yes, Your Majesty. We have gained a few more of those who can help heal the lands of your world." I said.

The king walked up and hugged me, with the queen following that up. Soon they were hugging everyone else as well.

Zane asked me, "This is the king and the queen of this entire city?"

I replied, "Actually, they are the king and queen of this entire region, including all of the lands where you are and out to where the giants' hometown used to be."

Carter said, "They seem so much like everyone else."

"I must agree with you. Every time we come to visit, they treat us like we are royalty." Bailey said.

Everyone was introduced and learned about each other. Meesha, Tasha, Burdock, Dohadie, and Datilina, were all talking with the queen. She seemed to love the conversation, it appeared.

After a reasonable time, the king asked me, "So what is it like in this new city on the mountain?"

"When we return, you are more than welcome to visit and view it, but now we need as many people as we can find to help trim trees and clear off roots, limbs, and branches that are now on the ground in large piles."

"Trees?" he asked.

"Yes. I feel we can use some of that lumber after it's cut for you, George, Oscar, and Ruther to create more wagons and homes. Then some of it will return to the city on the hill to create a few new homes there."

"It sounds like you must have a lot of trees for that to happen," he replied.

Bailey said, "Steve and Marty cleared off a good-sized section of the mountains trees and blew them into a pile at the foot of the hill."

"Well, that would be something to see," he replied.

Gram spoke out, saying, "I guess all your powers are coming to light."

Bailey replied, "Actually, it's not just Marty's powers as Steve and I, along with Vanessa and her sisters, have seen our powers increase as well."

"My goodness, all the stories I heard as a child are true," Gram said.

Haskin asked Zane, "How is it you know all about the history of our lands?"

"Your Majesty, centuries ago, Carter and I lived in that city on the mountain. Marty saved our entire city of people." Of course, as he said that, the king looked at me, and I was giving him a kind of a here-we-go-again look. But he continued to say, "Carter and I had died. However, it was Marty that brought us back to life again. We can tell you all the history of those times if you like."

"Of course," he replied.

But even as he answered that question, the king, queen, and everyone else looked at me with lots of uncertainty in those looks. Soon the king asked, "Care to join me for a few minutes?"

"But of course, Your Majesty," I replied.

"Did you bring with you a jester of some sort?"

"No, from all I know and what I have done, he speaks the truth," I replied.

"How was that even possible to bring them back to life? Better yet, how could you have saved their entire city so many centuries ago?"

I said, "It's a long story. However, it would be best if you keep in mind not all my powers can do such magnificent things. Since we entered Imperealisity, I have found new friends who can help me create some amazing events. But for now, we need to round up people from up here, then return to Lower Etheral, where Phil and some of the others are waiting for us, I am sure."

Averell had walked up just as I was saying that, and she asked, "Phil Danassia?"

"Yes, he is with others and getting horses and supplies," I replied.

"What do we need to do first?" the queen asked.

"First off, we need to walk outside the gates and see if we have people who can help us. Then we need to head down below," I said.

The king turned to one of the guards and asked, "Would you please get a few wagons ready to ride in?"

I raised my hand as I said, "Hold on. We won't need any wagons to go anywhere. We are going to walk."

The guards looked at me, and then it must have dawned on them what I was talking about.

The king said, "Well, if we need to walk out of the gates, let's do that." Soon all of us were seeing the gates open. Every one of us walked through those gates to be met by hundreds of other people.

All of us looked at them, then turned and looked at each other. I think all of us were amazed at the number of people who wanted to help.

It was John who walked up and stated, "I hope this is enough people to help with the trees and all other things that need to be accomplished around that city."

I replied, "John, that is a great number of people. Do they all know what it is that needs to be done?"

"I have told all of them we have piles of trees that need to have roots with dirt, limbs, and branches removed so we can run them through a mill. I have explained if they have horses, wagons, saws, and equipment to use, bring them. I also told them to bring bedrolls, blankets, and jackets and most of those things are in one of the wagons. Others who wish to go now know we are going to a city covered with vines, brush, and trees, and those things need to be removed as the city needs to be rebuilt," he replied.

I turned to face everyone in our group and said, "I guess we have a good number of people to help from up here. Your Majesty, if all of you wish to join us, you will have the chance to see another part of your region that I am sure you will love."

The king turned to one of the guards and asked, "Will you please tell the staff we will return soon."

"Yes, Your Majesty" was the reply.

Everyone was nodding their heads yes and sent up a cheer.

I looked over at Bailey and asked, "Care to open the door?"

As she opened the doorway to the area below, my grandmother walked up and asked, "Can I go with you?"

"Of course, you can, as I am sure Mom would love to see you."

Everyone walked out into the field below to find another large group of people, horses, wagons, and equipment sitting there waiting for us. Anthony walked up as we were walking out from up above and said to me, "It looks like we have an army of people to work on those trees and that town."

I said, "It seems we do. We will also be taking the king and queen, along with my grandmother and the elders, so they can see the city."

I walked over to Phil and asked, "Did we get all the food and tools needed along with rope?"

He started to walk over to one of the wagons they got, and as I followed him, he showed me a cart full of rope that had great lengths to them. "We also gathered up lots of saws and axes as well, along with plenty of food for everyone. In addition, one of these wagons has cleaning products, and another has bedding, towels, and even clothing for the people going and we now have extra horses," he replied.

"Great, is everyone here ready to travel?" I asked.

A cheer rose high enough that I'm sure it was heard on top of the mountain. People all yelled, "Yes!"

Steve asked, "Where to first?"

I looked at Bailey and asked her, "What do you think? The city first, and then we can find those who want to cut the trees down below?"

She replied, "I think that is a good idea as it will give everyone with us the chance to view the city."

Steve looked at both of us and then said, "So it's the city on the hill first."

Then a doorway opened.

CHAPTER 26

Feel the Excitement

People walked out into a world where there were thistles, brush, and trees as most of the vines had been burned off by Sky and Jasmin. They viewed buildings of great size and odd shapes, paths with trees growing up through them and growing out of the roofs of a few houses. It was as if the city had been taken over by nature, and now people arrived to take it back. We didn't want to remove all of nature, but we wanted to create a town again.

Anthony was talking to some of the people he rounded up, asking them to get things like blankets, clothing, towels, and bedding. He directed them to a safe section of the building where all those items could be placed until needed. We had already cleaned out a couple of buildings for supplies.

Nomi was gathering people and asking, "Who knows how to swing an ax?"

The king, queen, elders, and my grandmother all walked out and were met by our mothers. Everyone was looking all over the place at everything, as it was not something they had ever seen before. Our mothers were telling them about finding water and blasting trees down the side of the mountain.

The king asked them, "How did Marty bring those two back to life?"

"Carter was here in . . . I guess you might say a ghostly frozen state until Marty reached out and touched the door to the room where she had been left. As far as Zane, Marty found his bones and contacted the god of the dead and asked if he could bring Zane back, and it took some time, but he said he owed Marty a favor and made it happen," Catrina explained.

"Well, I guess this group has more power than all of us imagined," the queen said.

Wanda said, "We really don't know what all of their powers are, as it seems when people need help, their powers are simply there."

My mother said, "We have an idea of some of the things they can do and what they can create, but I feel if something needs building, fixed, saved, or healed in your world, all their powers will arrive as needed."

All of them discussed that Zane was a wise one and had sealed Carter in the room to keep her safe, but there were still many unanswered questions.

Anthony walked over and asked me, "Can we open a door down to the bottom of the hill?"

"Yes, we can, but we will probably only have time to move equipment down there and set up a camp before it gets dark. Do you want to set up a campsite down there and leave people there?" I asked.

"Well, do you think there is anything down there that can harm us?" Anthony asked.

"I don't feel anything dangerous if that is what you're asking. When we start working on those trees, we need to move a good number of them before all your people go to work on them." I commented.

"That's fine, let's take the wagons and equipment down and a few people now and the rest in the morning. How does that sound to you?" Anthony asked.

"We can move some of the wagons down there as I feel they will be safe overnight. I can move some of those trees if a few want to start working on them, but not after dark," I replied.

"Your Majesty, I need to leave for a bit with Steve and a few others. First, we need to check out the situation at the bottom of the hill. We need to move a few wagons down there as well. If you wish to join us, you can see all the trees Steve and I blew down the hill."

"Why don't we go with you, and then you may wish to return us home as it is getting to be evening," Haskin said.

"That will work out just fine as I wish to make sure everything is safe, and Steve can keep an eye on things until I return," I replied.

"Steve, care to open the doorway?" I asked.

Two of the four wagons that came from town lined up with a few people and equipment. Then, as Steve created the opening, all of us walked through. Even our mothers joined us this time with Gram. The only people left above were those working on clearing buildings and paths. Some people were chopping, raking, and removing debris, trees, and brush. Then we had those working on the hot-water lines with our blacksmiths.

Tasha and Meesha were walking with Medina and Majjeem behind one of the wagons and chatting away. The king and queen and the elders were all walking with me. We talked about all the trees that had been piled up in a massive area ahead of us.

The elders, king, and queen viewed the trees piled high with the queen stating, "All those trees look like one huge mountain."

Everyone was now standing and staring because to see all of these in this manner, it did look like another mountain.

I said, "Tony, why don't you place the wagons where you feel they will be safe, and I will move some of these trees. I need all of you to stand back because some of these may snap and shoot out branches. As a matter of fact, being behind a wagon might be a good idea."

Gram and our mothers all walked with the others behind the wagons for safety.

I asked Steve, "Can you stop any of those branches that fly this way?"

"I think I can probably blow them away as my power and strength is getting better."

"For right now, keep an eye open for anything flying that should not be heading our way, if you would, please."

I walked over and used my power to lift a tree off the others. I moved it to a location where people could work on it this afternoon or in the morning. Then I moved to the next one, then the next, and soon I had moved about a dozen trees off the pile and placed them in a safe location.

Everyone was standing back and watching the entire event. When I had finished, I turned, walked around, and everyone was standing there clapping. I stopped and took a bow, and then I heard lots of laughing.

"Alright, there are a few of those trees people can work on. We need to be very careful about removing any other trees. That means one of us should be down here, helping in any way we can," I said.

"We have a campsite to set up now. All of you who wish to stay down here tonight, let's get a campfire, some tents set up, and someone cooking up a meal while the rest of us go to work. We have the equipment, ropes, and saws to unload," Anthony said.

"We have a few tents and some of the others can use the wagons to sleep in, so a few of us will stay down here," one of the men from Anthony's crew stated.

Others were talking about setting up a campfire and fixing dinner. I looked around at those in our team, asking, "Is there one of you that wishes to stay for a short time while I take the king, queen, and elders home?"

A few of them agreed to stay. Dohadie, Datilina, Tasha, Meesha, Tom, and Art were making themselves comfortable.

Catrina said, "We can go back up above and make sure the fires are burning, and I think we need to see if they are fixing dinner as well."

"It would be nice to see how they are doing with that hot water as I am now ready for a nice bath," Mom said.

Gram looked at everyone around her and said, "Now that explains that terrible smell."

Mom asked, "What smell are you talking about, Mom?"

"You know that one from all of you who have not been taking showers or baths." Then she started laughing with the rest of those around her joining in.

"I'm just kidding, you know," she stated.

Bailey said, "When we are ready to take people back up to the top of the hill, we can walk over and check to see how they are doing at copying those drawings."

Steve stated, "I will remain here to be sure we don't have any problems."

Many of them got ready to head back to the city on the hill, while others were setting up this camp and getting ready to fix meals. I asked the king, queen, and elders, "Are you ready to return?"

"I think we are, Marty, as we have now seen a city that needs a huge amount of work but could be a wonderful place where people could live," the queen replied.

Carter and Zane walked up. Carter said, "Your Majesties and elders, it was a pleasure meeting all of you today. We look forward to revisiting sometime."

Zane added, "It will be wonderful to tell you about the people that lived here as they were hardworking, honest, and very wonderful men, women, and children. They were people from all walks of life and many kinds of people."

The queen said, "We will have to have Marty or his grandmother open a doorway so we can meet up again."

I stepped up and said, "If all of you are ready, I will open a door to the palace, and Bailey will be opening a door to the town on the hill above us."

Soon an opening was created in the city, with many people on our team walking back to the town. I opened an event. The rest of us walked back to the palace. As we reached the gates, they opened, and I walked with everyone back through them. After the gates closed, I said, "It was great to see all of you again." Then I looked over at my grandmother, walked up to her, and hugged her, saying, "I love you, Gram."

"I love you. I hope you come back soon," she replied.

"If any of you need us, you know how to reach us. I look forward to seeing all of you again soon," I commented.

As I said that, Haskin and Natalie both walked up and hugged me, with the queen saying, "Come back soon and stay safe."

Haskin said, "Thank you for the chance to see that city, as it is amazing as it is now, but I look forward to seeing it as it grows."

"I think it will be more amazing after it's cleaned up and rebuilt," I said.

"I think you're correct, and I do hope we see that," he replied.

My opening took me back to the base of that mountain.

CHAPTER 27

Setting Up Camps

As I walked out into the area around those fallen trees, I noticed many people set up a very nice campsite. I walked over and asked a few of them, "What do you have for water?"

One of the women turned and looked at me and said, "We heard the water out here is contaminated, so we filled containers before we left."

I replied, "That's good, but if you find you need more, we can take care of that. The city up above us has a well with good water, so we will see what we can do to ensure you have what you need."

As I was looking around, I noticed several people already hacking away at the limbs and branches on the trees I had moved off that pile. Others were taking the branches and cutting them up and making a pile of wood, like what we see at home when people sell cords of wood. Walking around where they were working, I noticed they already had about five of them stripped down to the main sections of the trees.

I spoke out and yelled, "I am going to move some of these."

As I reached out with my power, picked one up, and started to move it, a few people who did not hear what I said yelled and screamed, thinking something was attacking them. Then as I was moving it away from them, they noticed it was me.

I set all the ones they had already cleared off in a row to the side. Then I walked back over and said, "I will be back down here in the morning. In the meantime, you may wish to cut off those roots and remove all that dirt."

Steve walked up and said, "These people are working fools."

Art, Tom, and a few of the others from our team walked up, and Tom said, "I can't believe how fast all these people make light work of this project."

"You have seen nothing yet. Wait till you see what they did in that town of Lower Etheral. They built places for protection, about three of them in two to three weeks," Dohadie stated.

Some people walked over to the one I just placed and, about every ten feet, made a mark as to where to cut the tree. He was giving us log sections of about ten feet. As I was looking at them, I wondered if it would be a good idea to do that to all the trees, or should we cut them at different lengths?

Walking over to one of them marking a cut, I asked, "Is that so we can cut ten-foot lengths of lumber?"

He replied, "Yes, we have found that length works for most lumber that is cut because we can cut the lumber and then trim them to eight feet in length if we need them."

I asked, "How about cutting several of them this size, a number of the others eight and a few twelve feet in length as well? The reason I asked that is we can haul all those different lengths to our mill, and they can simply be cut without trimming them."

"That might work if we plan on creating buildings and homes with different-size lumber. We also need sizes for building the new wagons. I feel that is a good idea. Thank you," he replied.

"Well, that would create the lengths we need without wasting any lumber by trimming them," I replied.

One other man said, "We will wrap this up soon so all of us can eat, and we will start over again in the morning after we have breakfast."

Looking at Steve, I said, "Someone will return shortly to make sure you have protection if you need it down here." Then I created an opening. Steve and the rest of our group stepped through it.

As I walked out into the city, I found people all over the place and soon noticed many of our pets, mothers, and other team members headed my way. Bailey said, "We have been trying to make sure everyone has a place to sleep up here, and I hope they have room down below."

"I think they have that all figured out. I said someone should be down there in case there is trouble or need help," I replied.

Burdock and Steve were standing close by, and Burdock commented, "I can go down there if you open up one of those openings."

I replied, "I can do that, anyone going down there needs to get something to eat first."

Steve was looking over at Vanessa, as Vanessa said, "I am sure Steve, my sisters, our pets, and I can go down there and join Burdock. But I hope we have one of those old wagons to take down with us to sleep in."

Steve looked at me and said, "That will work and give all of us a good place to sleep."

Bailey and I looked around, and I said, "If anyone else who wishes to go down there for the night, speak up."

A few of the others seemed to brush it off, saying, "We have work to do up here," "I think I will just find a good place to sleep up here," and "We have a project to finish before we turn in."

"Steve, it's all up to you now, but if all of you are heading down there, you better eat before you go."

Burdock, Steve, Vanessa, her sisters, and pets all headed over to where they were cooking. It did not take long for all of them to eat and then return. Steve walked over to one of the old wagons we recovered from that long building. He waved at Heather, Krystle, and their pets, motioning them to join him. Soon, Burdock and Vanessa were there as well, and Steve was saying, "We can just push this through the opening and use it to sleep in tonight."

Burdock stated, "This is a sturdy wagon—that's for sure."

Vanessa said, "I think all of us need at least a sleeping bag tonight since we don't have a wagon full of straw."

Burdock joined in that conversation saying, "That may be a great idea."

Soon everyone had tossed their sleeping bags or bedrolls in the back of the wagon and grabbed up some water, then Vanessa opened the doorway. Some got in the front to guide the wagon, and the others pushed the old wagon through the opening.

Bailey and I walked over to our mothers, who were now standing there speaking to Medina, Carter, and Majjeem. Mom said, "Well, son, it looks like the king and queen found this place interesting."

"I think they did, and I got the feeling when I was taking them back the king was wishing he was here exploring with us," I replied.

Bailey said, "I checked on the women who are copying those drawings of the tunnels, pipes, and places the water goes to and they seem to be doing rather well. They were telling me that a few pages on the tops started to fall apart as they tried to move them off the others. While I was there one of them had a bag with her and pulled out a little bottle with a squeeze thingy on it and she sprayed the one page that looked like it would fall apart if moved, but after whatever she sprayed on that dried, she moved it with no problems."

"You know if we were at home, I bet hairspray or something like that would work," I said.

"It may be something of the same idea, but I never asked her what she uses it for," Bailey stated.

"I will have to walk over to that building tomorrow and see what people are talking about when it comes to burning boxes and tunnels," I said.

"I suppose we need to find out what everyone else is doing," Bailey said.

Many of us started walking back to the large open area that looked like it was a park of some kind at one time. Many others enjoyed working on small projects as they sat around on new benches and seats. Art walked up with Dohadie, Nomi, and Jack, followed by Tasha and Meesha, and I got the feeling all of them had been discussing moving on.

"Where is Steve?" Nomi asked.

"Burdock, Steve, Vanessa, her sisters, and pets all grabbed something to eat, their sleeping bags, water, and a wagon, and are now down with Anthony's crew," Bailey replied.

Nomi said, "Marty, I know this townsite is important, but we still need to find out what has happened further out west."

"I understand that. I feel we need to get everyone organized here. Then we can travel forward again."

All of us found a log that had been cut and trimmed and rolled it over to sit on with everyone else. Soon most of us were discussing the town site and moving forward. Catrina said, "I hate to just up and leave all these people here without protection and help if they need it."

About that time, I felt Carter getting excited and turned to see where she was looking. As Zane walked up to the group, he nodded his head as if for a greeting and found a place next to Carter to sit. "What's going on?" he asked.

Bailey said, "We were just thinking of moving on as we still have to find out what has been destroying the lands and homes west of here, and there is the matter of an excavation crew that seems to be missing."

Zane looked over at me, with a small grin and said, "Well, if anyone can find out what is happening and fix it, I am sure all of you will."

Nomi replied, "After all, I have seen and been through with this group, I have a feeling that is very true, Zane."

"Let's make sure everyone here has a place to sleep after we eat dinner," Majjeem said.

Manna yelled out, "Come and get it."

Soon, there was a line of people walking over to the area that had been cleared for the kitchen and dining. As Bailey started to get up, Tom said, "I'm going to run over and yell down into the tunnel where those furnaces and pipes are, so they know we're ready to eat."

"Tom, would you please tell the women working on those pages that food is being served and maybe one at a time could come over and eat so we have someone there at all times," Bailey asked.

"Sure thing," Tom replied.

Nomi yelled at his people who were getting supplies and putting other supplies in locations that would be out of the weather, saying, "If you want to eat, come and get it."

Soon everyone was gathering around and filling plates with food and settling down in places to eat. As we talked and discussed the town, all of us were speaking about different locations that would be good for sleeping.

Tom soon walked back with a woman I had not met yet, so I figured she was one of Egana's helpers. So, I asked, "Are you by chance one of the women who are trying to copy all those pages in the water building?"

"Yes, I am Glomera, and Egana is one of the others who recently located Nagana, and she is also helping," she replied.

"I'm Marty," I said.

"Oh, so it was you and someone else who made all that noise we heard, is that correct?" Glomera asked.

"I cannot lie. It was me, but I had help from Steve," I stated.

"Bailey told us a while ago when we got all that paper. Well, I guess I better get something to eat so I can get back there and let one of the others come to eat," she stated.

Ziggy, Agatha, Tabby, and Masher were walking by as she was talking and they stopped to hear what she was saying, then Agatha asked, "What if we go make sure no one enters that room and we let the others come and join you?"

"Have you eaten?" she asked.

Ziggy replied, "We have so, we will have them join you."

"That would be great as I am sure they are hungry as well. Thank you and tell them I am waiting for them, please," Glomera replied.

Soon two other women were walking over to Glomera, and all three of them headed to the food, filled plates, and sat down to eat.

It was not long before I noticed they were heading back past me and John, and I asked, "How are you doing with all those pages?"

Glomera and the other two stopped, with her saying, "I feel we have our work cut out for us. However, I believe the three of us can copy all those pages. Oh, and by the way, Marty, this is Egana, and this is Nagana."

"Well, Glomera, this is John." And as I looked at him, I said, "I think he's Nomi's foreman or man in charge when he is not around."

John nodded his head as he commented, "Nice to meet you, ladies."

I said, "If you need more help, please let us know. It has been nice meeting all of you, and I hope we can see what you're doing sometime tomorrow."

Soon dinner was over, and people were cleaning pots, pans, and the entire eating area, then everyone was gathering up blankets. Many of them wandered over near bonfires, as they figured they could sleep there. I heard one of them say, "If we start to get cold, we can wake up and put more wood on the fires."

John said, "I'm going to see if Nomi needs any help before everyone turns in, so I will see you tomorrow."

"I'm getting a bit tired myself. I may find some of the others and turn in as well. See you in the morning," I replied.

I looked around for Zane and Jack, found them, and walked over to where they were both talking. I figured it was probably wizardly things or something like that. As I approached them, they moved over to make room on a log so we could all sit and talk.

Zane said, "Well, I feel like Jack and I are new to the world of wise ones after seeing and knowing all the things you can do."

"Oh no, I'm no wise one or anything like that, but I do have a question for you," I remarked.

"What's that, Marty?" Zane asked.

"Carter was saying this mountain did not have fog for many years but when you learned of people coming, all of a sudden, it had lots of fog," I replied.

"Well, that is very true because when you showed up and warned us, I needed to make sure people were not seen easily, and creating that fog covered most of the city," he exclaimed.

I replied, "I wish you would not keep saying I showed up. I feel I did, now that I have had a few words with one of our other team members, but I can't explain it."

"It's okay, Marty. What is important is you were there, and you saved thousands of lives, and on top of that, you saved and brought back to life Carter and me."

"What about this fog?" I asked.

"This mountain is not as high as the other ones around us, and they never have had fog on them, but I created a spell to make it happen and now I can remove it. And I will because I feel this land is so different now than it was so long ago."

"Thank you, and do you feel you can protect all of those who stay when we leave?" Jack asked.

"I think so, Jack. For some reason, I feel my powers again, and I was teaching Carter before, and we can work together and set up a city council and people who make things happen. I am looking forward to seeing our city grow again," he replied.

Jack asked him, "Are you ready to remove the fog?"

"I am, Jack. Come with me and I will tell you how I created it and you will see how we remove it," Zane responded.

"I am heading to someplace to sleep, so I will see both of you in the morning," I commented.

"See you in the morning," I heard both of them reply.

Everyone was headed to wagons, coaches, or locations they found to fall asleep. It was weird as suddenly all the fog around us vanished. I said, "I guess Zane removed the spell for the fog."

Bailey looked at me and then at the sky and asked, "How did he do that?"

"Tell you later, gator. For now, let's get some sleep." We both decided we needed to use the sleeping bags, and it wasn't long before we had slid into them, and our pets were now in animal form, joining us on top or around us. Soon everyone seemed to be asleep.

CHAPTER 28

Morning

I turned and snuggled up to Bailey, and she wrapped her arm around me. Then she kissed me. I wrapped my arm over hers and pulled her close, and I said, "Bailey, I love you and wish we could stay just like this forever."

Suddenly I heard, "Hey, are you talking to me?"

I shook my head, pulled back, and then opened one of my eyes to see Bailey in the sleeping bag next to mine, and she was raised with one arm bracing herself so she could view me.

I looked at her and shook my head again, then opened both eyes and said, "I just had the greatest dream. I woke up to you and then you woke me up again."

"Well, pardon me. What was that about?"

"You and I were sleeping in what must have been both of our sleeping bags zipped together. I had just turned over and felt you wrap your arm around me, and then you kissed me."

"Wow. That sounds like a great dream to me," she replied. Then she reached over and wrapped her arm around me and kissed me. This time I said, "Wow. Now I need to make sure I am not still dreaming. That was a wonderful moment."

We pulled each other close, and suddenly, we had company. Tabby was jumping upon us, with Ziggy pressing against my back as if to snuggle up to my sleeping bag.

"Okay, alright all ready, you two win. We're getting up," I said.

As we were getting up and climbing down from the wagon, we noticed an opening had been created, but it was just around the other side of the carriage next to us, and we could only see a small portion of where it was coming from. I had an idea of who it was, as I felt him, but was not sure if it was only one person. So, all of us walked over to see who was joining us.

As we walked past the next wagon, the entrance suddenly closed, and all of us stood there looking around to see who had arrived. I sent a thought to Steve: *Hey, bud, was that you that just arrived up here?*

What are you talking about? You just woke me up, he replied.

Sorry. I thought you were with the person who just arrived.

We will be up there in a bit, so save us some breakfast if you would please.

You got it, I replied.

Suddenly, I knew my feelings were correct about who it was because not only could I feel him, but as I turned, I looked at my father and said, "Hey, how did you know where to find everyone?"

"Oh, that was easy, as your grandmother asked me to visit the opening between worlds so she could create an opening to let me have a look at this place while she was here visiting," he replied.

I asked him, "You brought Mark and Robert as well?"

"Yes, both are here as well. Mark and Robert walked over to find their wives," he replied.

As Bailey heard that, she asked, "Dad's here?"

My father pointed over to where Catrina was standing and now hugging Robert. So she headed over to see her father and say hello. When she got there, everyone was chatting up a storm.

No. There was no real storm. It was just a figure of speech.

Dad and I walked over and joined all the others and were soon listening to all the conversations.

Mark asked, "Where is Steve?"

Bailey said, "He's down at the bottom of the hill. But Marty just spoke to him, and he said he would be up soon and wanted breakfast."

"Well, we will just surprise him then," Mark replied.

Catrina and Robert were talking about this city. He was saying, "I have never seen anything like this before. Well, except on one of those Indy what's-his-name movies."

Catrina said, "There are a lot of things going on here that will spin your mind around."

Of course, all three of our fathers were standing there, listening to what Catrina was saying. My mother and Steve's mother were there as well. Bailey said, "Dad, you won't believe the things that have happened since we came to this city."

I asked, "Bailey, how about we let all our parents talk while we sit back and just watch?"

"You're probably correct as I know my mom would love to bend my father's ear about what's been going on," she replied.

Before you ask, no ears were bent in any direction.

"We have seen Marty and Steve both clear off the entire side of a mountain of trees. And Marty brought two people back from the dead," Catrina continued.

"They did what?" Mark asked.

"Both of my visions came into play here. I viewed both of those happenings. First, Marty brought a woman who was only bones in that tower over there back to life." She was pointing to the building where we found Carter.

"He brought bones back to life?" Robert asked.

"That was not all of it because later Marty brought back the man that woman loved. They are now a couple, as they were before they died. You will also have to see all those trees at the bottom of the hill in a pile and learn about how our daughter and Vanessa have grown in power."

My father looked at me, then asked, "How in the world did you bring anyone back from the dead?"

Mom looked at him and asked, "Do you remember that tall tale about Anubis back at their base camp?"

He replied, "Well, of course, I do. I found that to be interesting but far-fetched."

Mom said, "You may wish to think again about that being far-fetched. You see, all of us have now actually seen Anubis, and he is who Marty contacted to bring Zane back to life."

"And who is Zane?" Mark asked.

Wanda replied, "It's a long story, but to cut it short, he was the wizard or, as they say here, the wise one, who saved the people of this city and the woman he loved, who is named Carter."

I spoke out and said, "I now hear Bailey and Vanessa have been working out, because we heard they opened doors on a water house Nomi and others could not."

"Wow, anything else new and exciting since we have been gone?" Robert asked.

"Well, we have a few new friends now that are with us that have powers of their own," my mother stated.

"What kinds of powers?" Dad asked.

"I get the feeling one of them can manipulate time. One is the goddess Medina that Marty told us about sometime back. I understand the other is your TV hero," my mother replied.

He looked at her and asked, "Superman? Iron Man? Who?"

"No, dear. Who is the god that has a huge hammer and can bring lightning from the sky?"

"Thor?" my father asked.

"Yes, that is Thomas Thorborn, the one over talking with Nomi."

My father, Mark, and Robert turned and looked at him, my father saying, "No way."

"You're kidding, correct? That is really Thor?" Robert asked.

Mark said, "All of what you're telling us seems so unrealistic."

Bailey spoke out, saying, "Not kidding, Dad, as we saw him change."

"What about the one who can work with time? Who is that?" Mark asked.

"That would be Art. He is the one standing and watching the kids shoot at that target," Wanda replied.

"Medina was the ghost that Marty said scared the daylights out of him, correct?" Dad asked.

"She is the young girl sitting over by Meesha, Tasha, and Majjeem near the guards' coach," Wanda said as she pointed to where they sat.

Our fathers were now looking at each other and back at the people we just spoke of and then back at each other again, shaking their heads.

As our fathers were all standing and learning all about our new magical and marvelous heroes, Dad asked, "We had the chance to meet all of them when they came to Earth to visit, didn't we?"

"Yes, you did, but they were only showing you what they wanted you to see," Mom replied.

"So all of them have different kinds of powers. What are they all doing here?" Mark asked.

"Well, Medina was here on this planet protecting the forests and animal life. Tom and Art arrived because they said the timeline had become disrupted. Tom told us one of those reasons had already been discovered, and that was our group of travelers. However, all of us feel there is more," my mother replied.

"Well, to be honest with you, just about every one of our kids and pets, including Vanessa, her sisters, and their pets, has shown us their powers. So to some degree, I feel when all of them started using those powers, that alone might have caused the timeline to change," Wanda added.

"We all know they have been using their powers, but was that enough to create a shake-up in the timeline of this planet?" Mark asked.

I replied, "We have been using our powers ever since we stepped into this world, and later, we had to travel up, over, and through huge sand dunes. In one valley, we were all stopped by sand being blown up in the air with scorpions coming out of the ground."

Robert asked, "All of you stopped for a large number of little scorpions?"

Mark said, "I used to simply brush them off my shirt when I was younger."

Bailey said, "Oh, those were not little by any means, as most of them stood as tall as our little protectors here in human form and were as long as we are tall," and she pulled Tabby up close to her as she said that.

I continued, "What happened next was unreal as they had all our wagons and coaches surrounded and more of them were coming out of the ground. Every one of the soldiers was using their swords on them. Every kid that could use a bow was hitting their targets. Sophia, Vanessa, her sisters, and pets were showing new powers we had never seen before."

"Yes, everyone who had powers was using them, including Jack, Majjeem, and the three of us," Mom added.

"Burdock and the Denarians were all doing what they could to protect the wagons and people. Finally, after a good long time, we started to see them stop coming out of the sand," Wanda said.

Catrina added, "Every one of us used our powers that day. I think some of our powers have grown just like our kids' powers have."

All of us turned as a new doorway opened. Steve, Vanessa, her sisters, and pets were walking through, followed by Burdock and a few people from down below.

Steve said, "I knew you were here. Marty woke me this morning and said something about an opening, but then I suddenly felt you were here."

"It seems your powers are increasing," Mark said.

"I think all of our powers are increasing, Dad," he replied.

Everyone in our team gathered around and shook hands, gave hugs, and talked about how nice it was to see each other again, while others from the camp were walking over to learn more about those they had not met yet. A good number of the people who came from Etheral had not met our fathers the previous time. So everyone was now learning about our parents.

Zane, Carter, Art, Tom, and Medina all walked up to us. I introduced them to our fathers. Conversations were all over the map about all the recent events.

No, there was no map laid out. No one was walking all over a map. This is just another way of saying those conversations were all over the place.

Everyone was now talking about bringing back the dead, saving the town, finding the city, and of course, the powers of our new friends.

I found myself amazed at some of the questions our fathers had. But I think they were learning more about the powers we now had, compared to when they saw us last time.

"Art, I understand you might be able to manipulate time, is that correct?" Mark asked.

"Well, I guess, to some degree I can. I am a traveler that goes to all planets to learn about how lives progress and what their history has been," Art replied.

"You're saying you can travel to all the planets that have life on them?" he asked.

"Yes, our society is designed to keep an eye on events in the universe, while we try to make sure things don't get out of control and destroy the universe."

"What could destroy everything we have?" Robert asked.

Art said, "Let's just look at your world. How many wars have you had because of selfish people of wealth and outlandish religious beliefs since the start of your planet?"

"I would probably say every one of them. Most of those wars were because people felt they were better than everyone else and even convinced a handful of followers to yell in favor of war," Dad said.

Art replied, "I think you're correct. But you must always keep in mind the ones that were greedy and narcissistic. People like that always feel they are right, and everyone else is wrong. So they use all kinds of remarks to put others down and eventually do whatever it takes to take control of other people's lives. But of course, as they do things like that, each of them becomes more capable of creating bigger events, which can lead to the planet's total destruction."

"Tom, I hear you are more than just Thomas Thorborn," Dad said.

"I guess you might say that, but it's probably best we don't promote that," he replied.

I mentally said to Dad, *It would not be suitable for everyone here to know who they are and how they look.*

167

I understand, son.

"Well, Tom, I am pleased to meet you as I hear you're one of my heroes."

"Well, that's interesting, as I'm not sure I am anyone's hero."

"Well, on our planet Earth they have movies about you," he replied.

Medina heard that and said, "That's what I hear too."

"Oh yes, movies, I have heard about those and caught a glimpse of one when we were on your planet," Tom replied.

"Tom, how about you and Art come with me for now?" I asked.

Tom looked over at Medina, and she was kind of grinning and nodding her head. Then he looked over at me and said, "That might be a good idea."

"Sorry, guys, I had to get both of you out of there, or the next things we might have seen would have been both of you change and scare the hell out of people," I said.

So as we walked along, Tom was asking, "Was I a hero in all those movies?"

"Well, Tom, I have seen a few shows or movies that you are in as a hero," I replied.

Art replied by saying, "In many worlds today, they have pictures that run in sequence, so it creates something that looks like they are moving as in real life. Oh, and by the way, I have seen someone play Thor in one of those movies on Marty's planet."

"Oh, we saw that on what they called a TV at Marty's home. What do you think, did he look like me?" Tom asked.

Art looked at him and then over at me, shook his head, then looked back at Tom, saying, "You know, I think that guy that was playing your part looked more like a god of thunder than you do."

Tom looked at both of us as we started laughing, and then he gave us one of those squinty-eyed looks like Tabby used to give me all the time. "Alright, now I know you're kidding because no one is a better Thor than me."

I said, "I don't know, but I guess when we get done over here, we can travel home, and I will pull up more of those movies to show you."

"You can do that? I mean, just do as you say, pull up one of those movies to watch?"

"Tom, you two already know I can do amazing things," I declared.

Bailey walked over with Steve, Vanessa, and our pets as all of us were laughing. Steve said, "I don't think I even want to know."

I said, "I told Tom when we go home again, he can join us, and I will show him more movies about Thor. Art was just telling him the guy who played his part looked more like Thor than he does."

Bailey said, "Oh, that will be interesting, him watching a movie about himself."

Ziggy asked, "Do they really have a movie about him and his hammer?"

"We sure do," Steve replied.

"When we all get done over here, I want to see some of those movies too," Ziggy commented.

I said, "I think Medina was surprised to see him on TV when we were all there. Because when we first met, I told her they had movies about Thor, and I think the way she said it was 'That figures, he's such a ham.'"

CHAPTER 29

Projects Happening

With everyone finished eating breakfast and having conversations about everything you can imagine, our fathers decided to work with Magness and Staggerus and see if they could get the hot-water ovens working and locate places to take a hot bath.

Our mothers and some of the others were following workers as they cleared places near old buildings and wanted to see if they could be usable again. A good number of the homes looked like they might still have sound walls, but where there were wooden shingles and slats, many of them needed replacing.

Zane and Carter gathered up Tasha, Meesha, and Majjeem along with a few others, and all of them worked on clearing more paths that simply had lots of brush.

Many of Nomi's men were now searching buildings to see if they had functional areas we could use for people to take showers or baths.

Steve and I opened a doorway to the location at the bottom of the hill. A few of us walked down to help get the trees moved and placed for them to trim and cut to size. Ziggy and Max were walking at our sides. We noticed a good number of trees that had already been trimmed and cut into three different sizes.

Ziggy asked, "Why don't we open the door to the beach area near the pond and just roll those into the pond so they can start working on them?"

"I gather you mean the pond near the sawmill," I replied.

Steve said, "I'm not so sure we can make an opening wide enough to accommodate some of those logs. But I guess we can try."

I looked around and located Anthony. Walking up to him, I said, "You know I am so used to calling you Tony, I sure hope you don't mind."

"Not at all. Most people do call me that."

"Good. Would you please do me a favor and round up about four men and at least two horses so we can open a door and pull a few of those logs through it at a time?"

"Sure," As he made that statement he walked over to a group of men that looked like they were resting. Soon he had two of them walking back with him, and two others were walking over to get a couple of horses.

When everyone was with us and the horses and ropes arrived, we discussed how we would open a door near that pond, pull the logs over to it, and then just roll them into the water.

Steve said, "We will have to simply move them near the water's edge and then give them a push into the pond."

"I'm hoping they are ready to cut this number of trees," I added.

Soon, two men grabbed one end of the rope, giving it a wrap around a couple of trees. Two of the others were getting ready to lead the horses through the door we would soon open.

Anthony asked me, "Did you know Sky and Jasmin are down here?"

I looked at him and said, "I felt them but was not paying attention to where they are. Just a minute, let me look around and I will find them." As I was looking in places that seemed a bit away from the people and wagons, I noticed both and they looked like they were sound asleep. However, if they are like most animals, like my pet Ziggy, they probably have one eye open.

Steve was looking all around, so I asked him, "Do you see them?"

"I'm not sure, but I do notice a variation in the landscape over there." He pointed in the direction I knew they were located.

"That's where they are," I replied.

I sent a thought to Sky and asked, *Are you two doing well?*

We are well. We landed here early this morning, and Anthony noticed our landing and came over to chat with us. He was telling us all about what they are doing down here. I see they have a lot of work already done.

They do. We need to move all those trees they have ready over to our base camp for the lumber mill.

Well, you have fun. We are going to catch up on some sleep.

You stay safe, and we can talk later.

Speaking to Steve, I said, "They got here this morning."

"I figured that because they were not here last night."

"Alright, let's rope up these logs one or two at a time and move them," Anthony yelled.

Steve created an opening right beside the pond about twenty feet away. The horses were used to move two logs this time straight ahead alongside the pond, then they were untied. I used some of my power to roll them into the lake. Some of the men from our base were shifting logs around already in the pond. As they noticed us, they advanced over to where all of us were pushing the first two logs into the pond.

"Marty, it looks like you are bringing us a gift," one of the men said.

"I am. We have a lot more," I replied.

He looked back past me and noticed hundreds of trees all stacked in a gigantic pile and said, "Wow, I guess you do."

"Would you please get more help on moving these as we are going to be bringing over many more?" I asked.

One of the men climbed out of the boat and ran over to Mathew Gaspard, the one person who had been working to make sure our mill runs the way it should. Soon they gathered a few others and walked over to us.

"Mat, it's good to see you again," I said.

"Well, it's good to see you again too. So what do you have for us?" he asked.

"Please walk with me as we have a whole mess of trees. We are trimming all the branches and roots off, and they are cutting them to lengths of eight, ten, and twelve feet." Both of us walked back to where we were getting the logs. He was amazed at the massive pile of trees and their size.

"Wow. How did all those trees end up in such an enormous pile?" he asked.

"Well, that's a long story, but to keep it short, Steve and I stood at the top of this mountain and blew them all down here."

"What?" he asked.

Steve, who was standing there keeping the doorway open, said, "What he just told you is what we did."

"Mat, this is what we plan on doing. We move and trim all the trees, then cut them to length. After we shift them to the mill, all of you can cut them into two-by-fours, two-by-six planks, four-by-fours, and maybe even one by ones. We need to have lumber for homes at the base, lumber to create new coaches, and lumber for homes up there on the top of that mountain." As I said that, I pointed to the top of the hill.

"Well, one thing for sure, it seems you have enough trees to keep us busy for a long time, and I feel we may need to enlarge our method of cutting," he replied.

"The king will be paying us, so we can pay all of you a wage for doing all the work," Steve said.

I said, "Our fathers are here, and I may be able to have them work with you on getting a larger setup created."

"Whatever you want to do is fine with me. Just give us a road map of the things needed and how you need them cut."

Soon, Mathew and I were standing, watching as horses were dragging logs to the water's edge, where I used my power and just gave them a push into the water. Then, I looked at Steve and asked, "How are you doing at holding that doorway open?"

"I am fine. We only have about two more to go," Steve said.

Soon all the logs were floating in the pond. Steve and I said our goodbyes to Mathew and his crew, as we walked back through the doorway to piles of trees. Walking over to Tony, I said, "We need to remove a few more off that pile, so please ask everyone to step back. I will take care of that."

Anthony yelled to the people, "I need all of you over here now."

Soon many people were walking our way, and those who were the last were looking over their shoulders to make sure no one was left behind. Steve and I walked over to that massive pile of trees, and I started to move them and roll them from top to bottom. Once we had about a dozen more of those separated from that larger pile, we made sure people could now work on them safely.

Steve and I walked over to Sky and Jasmin, and I said, "I hope you have found good food around here."

"We have been filling up on lots of greens and are good," she disclosed.

"Well, we need to return above for now, so we may be back down here shortly to move more of those trees."

"Well, for us, this is rather nice as we have friends around us, and it seems very safe," Jasmin remarked.

Steve and I turned and stood there looking at the trees that were just moved, and Steve said, "Some of those are so big around. How will Mat even get them cut?"

"I'm not sure, but from what he was saying, it will be possible, so I told him maybe our fathers could help with a way to do that. One good thing is those trees are not as huge as a number of those in other sections of the mountain," I replied.

Soon, Steve and I were stepping out near the open field at the top of the hill. As we looked around, we could see everyone busy chopping down brush, weeds, and vines, and some were removing trees in roadways and paths. Tom and Medina walked up to us. Medina said, "We were just going to walk over and see what's happening in that boiler-room area. Care to join us?"

"I think our fathers are over there helping. Let's go," I replied.

Steve said, "I think I will find Vanessa and see what she's doing."

"Go for it, you know where we will be," I said.

Steve wandered off, and I could see him waving at Vanessa, who must have been working with our mothers and a few others clearing brush. Soon the three of us were at the building where they found the furnaces. We walked in and heard everyone down inside the hole in the ground. Since I had not seen what was down there, I was curious and said, "I guess we go down there and see what's happening."

Medina was heading over to the girls copying maps.

They placed torches and a box of matches in a location easy to reach, and I grabbed one, handed the other to Tom, and lit them. Soon we were climbing down the ladder to a large area with pipes running in all directions. We could hear people talking to our right, left, and down the tunnel ahead of us. I felt my father was off on our right, so I started heading down that way. Soon, I was standing and watching my dad and Magness working on a pipe that looked like it was leaking. They were talking away, and I could feel my father knew I was there. So I said, "Yes, I am here."

He started laughing and asked, "Can you tell me what I feel?"

"As a matter of fact, yes," I replied.

"How is the tree trimming and cutting going?" Dad asked.

"It's going well, and we have already moved a couple of those huge ones to the pond, but I'm not sure how Mat will cut those that size. Other than that, I do have a few questions for you," I asked.

"What's on your mind?" he said.

"We have been considering moving farther west to see if there really is a problem out there. We figure if you, Mark, and Robert are here, and our mothers wish to stay, we can travel, then we can always jump back here since we know where this location is and where we need to open our doorway."

"Well, we have a good amount of time off from our jobs, so we can help over here, and it won't be as much time at home in comparison," Dad replied.

"Great, we can discuss this later this evening with all of the others and see what they think as well," I declared.

Suddenly, a voice was in my head, and I heard Steve reaching out to me.

Marty, Vanessa and I, along with her sisters and pets, are going to visit her parents. She wants to ask her parents if they wish to visit with ours since we are all together. So give us a shout if you need us for anything, Steve said.

Okay, just stay safe, I replied.

"Well, Dad, it sounds like Steve and Vanessa are going over to see her parents and may bring them back with them," I commented.

Dad replied, "It would be nice if they did come back over here as he wanted some of that lumber, and he was talking about making an arrangement with the king for those coaches."

"So are those big round containers used to heat the water?" I asked.

Magness said, "Those are big wood-burning water heaters."

"Well, maybe we better make sure to keep some wood for these," I replied.

Dad spoke out saying, "What would help is if we had some kind of solar power system for those."

Magness looked at him by tipping his head down as if looking over glasses that he didn't have. Then Dad said, "I will explain later," and then both laughed.

"How long are you two going to stay down here working on these pipes?" I asked.

Magness replied, "We have a lot of these connections to check, and we have found a few places we need to shut off the water because of bad pipes. But I don't think we will have to replace a lot of them."

"We are heading back upstairs as I can feel Bailey, Medina, and the women who had been copying all the drawings and want to check those out," I said.

Tom and I walked into the room where the women were creating drawings of the old pages. Medina and all the girls seemed to be engrossed in what they were looking at. Bailey sent me a thought saying, *It would be so much easier if we could use a camera, photograph all of these, and go home and have prints made.*

I must agree with you on that. It looks like some of these may not make it, I said.

Tom was walking all around the room viewing the cubbyholes filled with papers and said, "Some of these papers over here don't look too bad."

Egana, Glomera, Nagana, and Bailey looked up from what they were doing and over to where he stood, with Egana saying, "Many of those are copies of what was here, but only in the one row next to that desk. We have placed copies in all the boxes except those top four that you're looking at."

I walked over to where Tom was standing as Medina was over by the four girls and I looked over Tom's shoulder, asking, "So we can take one of these out and look at it?"

"Yes, but only the ones in that row as the rest of those rows have all got to be pulled out and gently copied," Bailey said.

As both of us stood there looking at what they had copied, our mouths were open and then we looked at each other, and I said, "This looks like that building where the water valve is located, and that has to be the pipe that runs from there to over here."

He replied, "I feel you're correct, and if all of those papers are like this, whoever is left here will have a very informative view of all the water lines and where they go."

We put the paper we removed back in the cubby. Tom and I walked over and joined the others watching them as they worked, and Medina commented, "You ladies are doing a fantastic job here."

Tom and I were listening, and Tom added, "We are impressed with how many papers you have already copied."

I added, "Yes, very impressed. But I feel we must return to the center of the city. So please be sure to let one of us know if you need anything."

"We will let you know. All of us feel this is more fun than work," Glomera replied.

CHAPTER 30

Talking About Moving On

Tom, Bailey, Medina, and I walked out of the room and headed back to the center of town, and we were talking about the results of what those girls were doing. The four of us found their drawings to be better than the originals they copied. We noticed some of the other members of our crew and walked over to where they were chatting away.

I was hearing them discuss the idea of moving west, and I said, "We will have a meeting this evening and be talking about those who can stay here and those who will want to travel forward."

Nomi asked, "What if some of our people wish to stay here and try to create a life here?"

Carter and Zane had been there listening to everyone. Zane said, "If you have people who wish to live here, Carter and I feel it would be wonderful to see this town alive again."

I looked at him and then back to Nomi and said, "I think you have your answer."

"Sounds like we need to gather people from down below and have them join us so we can find out who wants to stay and who wants to move on," I said.

Bailey asked, "Do you want to get Steve and go down below?"

"Steve and Vanessa are at her parents' home right now. He told me a while ago that they were heading over there to see if they wanted to join all of us. I get the feeling Vanessa spoke with her mom already," I replied.

"Does anyone care to join us as we go back down below and talk to Anthony and his people?" I asked.

We heard several replies, but most were from people who were busy cleaning up nearby buildings, saying, "We have more to do here before we take a break."

One other person who came from Etheral in Anthony's group replied, "Maybe later, but right now, our group is pretty busy getting ready to cut down a few trees up here."

Tasha, Meesha, and Majjeem joined us, with Majjeem asking, "Can we go along with you?"

I said, "Yes, you can. Anyone who wants to go down the hill at this time, please join us over here."

"Majjeem, do you know where we are going?"

"I do, as I noticed where you went before," she replied.

"How would you like to create the opening for us?"

I could feel her getting excited and then heard, "Oh yes. Yes, I can do that."

"Jack, are you and Burdock going with us?"

"We're coming," Jack replied.

The doorway opened, and about twenty of us walked through, and then Majjeem closed it behind us. Looking around for Anthony, I spotted him a reasonable distance away with a rope around a few trees high up on the pile. The other end of the rope was tied to a horse down below.

Everyone needs to keep in mind that some of these trees are huge and others are smaller but all of them have tons of dirt all around the roots.

Nomi walked up to me and said, "That sure doesn't look safe to me."

"I think I have to agree with you," I replied.

We started to walk over, and it was just about the time we got close, I got a terrible feeling. That feeling was coming from a massive pile of trees in front of us about to move. I yelled, "Anthony." Suddenly many of the trees began to roll out at the bottom, and most of them on the top began to fall. Anthony was plummeting with all of them.

Bailey and I ran up to the edge of the pile. Bailey ran over to the horse and set it free of the rope and created a colossal shield, and I reached out with my powers and grabbed Anthony just as one of the trees was about to crush him into another one. Pulling him toward us, I felt others behind us running up. Jack and Majjeem suddenly produced powers that seemed to help hold back the trees coming our way.

Tasha, Meesha, and Burdock were yelling at people to move and get out of the way.

Jack yelled, "Do you have him?"

I replied, "I have him, but we need to hold those trees."

"You get him safe, and we will see if we can help hold these trees in place until you can help." Jack replied.

Majjeem said, "If we can, walk back slowly, allowing some to move down that may help. But we need to do it soon because we can't hold those in place for very long. I can't do much here as I'm just not that strong."

I turned and placed Tony well away from any harm, then I looked at Bailey, Jack, and Majjeem, saying, "Tony is safe. Let me see what I can do with those trees as all of you back up and away from them."

"That sounds good to me," Jack replied, and I noticed Bailey and Majjeem nodding their heads yes as well.

All of us began walking back fast away from that huge pile of tumbling trees. As we got a good way back, I stated, "All of you need to move back out of the way so I can use more of my power on those trees." Using my power to slow the progress of that load of trees falling toward us, I felt we now had it under control.

I looked at Jack and Majjeem and Bailey, stating, "The three of you just helped to stop a real problem."

Soon, I had a good number of trees spread out in different places where people could trim and cut them to length.

Anthony was brushing himself off and twisted his head as if to get kinks out of his neck. Then when he started looking around, he walked over and said, "I'm sure happy you didn't let that tree crush me."

"It was about to—that's for sure. It seems I'm always trying to make sure you don't get crushed by trees. It looks like we came down here just in time. So what the heck were you doing up there?"

Anthony stated, "You know some of these trees are huge. I thought I could get up on one of the larger ones and toss a rope over another one near it, then just climb back down and be safe."

"Tony, most of these trees are all loaded with tons of dirt and mixed in with small trees and larger ones and you really can't tell which ones are loose or not," I replied.

"Our people have been cutting and trimming trees so fast, and I just wanted to make sure they had more of them off that pile. I didn't want any of them getting hurt trying to bring them down to the ground level," he said.

"Oh, good job, get yourself killed in the process, showing them what not to do. From now on, please let those who can move those trees safely do it. We all have something to do here we are good at, and I'm afraid you're not good at flying," I replied.

Anthony nodded his head and commented, "I won't argue about that."

A doorway opened with Steve, Vanessa, her parents, sisters, and pets walking toward us a short distance away. Vanessa's mom and dad were both looking all around, and her father said, "Marty, that's one heck of a massive amount of trees piled up there and many tons of dirt with it."

"Yes, it is, George. There is so much dirt on those roots that I think we will have another mountain near us soon. But we do have a lot of wood to cut up, and I'm glad you two could join us, as our parents are all here as well," I replied.

"That's what Steve and Vanessa were telling us. But they wanted us to see all the trees you and Steve brought down the side of that mountain. I must admit that's one heck of a way to topple down trees," George replied.

"About ten minutes ago, you could have watched a few of us trying to save Anthony from being crushed by some of those trees." As I said that, I looked over at Anthony and gave him a very disappointed look.

"What happened?" Steve asked.

"Anthony was trying to show all of the workers down here how not to climb up on a pile of unstable trees," Jack stated.

Bailey added, "He was trying to tie a rope on a few at the top of the pile to pull more down and almost got crushed."

Majjeem spoke out, saying, "We all know he intended to help the people, but we almost lost him."

Anthony followed all of that up with "If it had not been for them, I would now be pushing up starpets."

"Starpets?" Bailey asked.

April spoke out, saying, "Bailey, many years ago when George and I visited your planet, Marty's parents, Marie and Fred, were driving us around Walla Walla, and we passed a huge place with lots of stones with writing on them and statues all over. When we asked him about what we were viewing, Fred replied, 'That's where many people who have passed are now resting.' Then he explained where people go when they die.

"I noticed a good number of flowers like what we call starpets, and I mentioned that by saying, 'It's amazing to see so many starpets and how well they are taken care of.' Of course, your mother asked what I was talking about, and I answered her by saying, 'All of those beautiful flowers.'

"Marie told me at that time what I was viewing were called daisies."

"Now I understand. Pushing up daisies and pushing up starpets are the same." Bailey commented.

"Correct," April replied.

"Anthony, sorry, but you need to stick around. We will get the trees you need. All you must do is yell," Steve said.

"I know, and I was simply having a time of stupidity. But some of the people were saying they were running out of trees to trim, so being the hero I am, I told them I would take care of it."

Steve stated, "I'm just glad like everyone here that you're still with us and not, as you say, pushing up . . . what did you call daisies?"

"You mean starpets," he replied.

"Yes, I'm glad you're not pushing up starpets," Steve said.

"Steve, let's make sure all these people have enough trees to trim for a good day, and then we should go back up top," I commented.

Soon all of us were directing people to safe locations. Suddenly, I heard someone yell, "What the heck is that?"

I turned and looked around, and what others could not see, I did see, and someone just walked into a dragon.

I started laughing and said, "Jasmin, please show yourself so no one else here will run into a solid wall."

Jasmin said, "I'm sorry I was sound asleep. I do hope you're all right."

The man who ran into her was now looking into the eye of a dragon and stepped back about five feet, then said, "Wow, Jasmin, I have never seen you that close before, and I sure never saw you before walking into you."

"Are you well?" she asked.

"Oh yes, I am fine. It sure was a sudden stop, however." Then he started laughing, and many others around him joined in.

Jasmin stated, "I'm happy you are not hurt."

Bailey, Majjeem, and Jack walked over to me, and as they arrived, I said, "What the three of you did was impressive. I could not have held back those trees and saved him. Thank you."

"One thing we found is our powers seem to be growing," Jack said.

Majjeem added, "Yes. I must agree because I could never do that kind of thing before."

I looked at Bailey and said, "Your shield is three times the size it was the first time I saw it."

"I know for some reason I can now create one that covers a larger area," she replied.

"Well, I am pleased to hear that, because that may mean the three of you will always have those powers and skills," I added.

Bailey asked, "Are we like a battery to others?"

"You mean because those around us are gaining more powers?" I asked.

She stood there as if thinking about something, looking at nothing in particular, then looked back at me and said, "It seems we have gained powers and many of those around us who normally would not have a lot of power are gaining more. So is it us, or is it all of us?"

"Maybe it's Mother Nature, as they say," I replied.

After moving and spreading out over a dozen trees, I looked around and found Anthony and asked him, "Do you have enough trees now?"

"I feel we do at this time, but these people are hard workers, and I would imagine all of these will be trimmed and cut before the day's end."

"Let us take care of moving them. We can't afford to lose you," I replied.

"Steve, I need to figure out how we can move on and still make sure these people are safe. If we had not shown up when we did, Anthony would have been as flat as a slice of bread pounced on by a one-ton gorilla."

Tony looked at me and was shaking his head with a bit of a frown on his face, then he asked me, "What is a one-ton gerla?"

"A one-ton gorilla is a huge furry animal that has features of a human in a way and can be found in forest areas," I replied.

"I see. So if he was jumping up and down on me, he would make me as flat as one of those trees smashing me to nothing?"

Steve spoke out and replied, "Tony, I think you got the idea."

"Tony, can you please gather your people and join us as we head up topside?"

"Well, let me shake myself out a bit more, as that last little adventure was too close for comfort," he replied.

CHAPTER 31

Time for Choices

"Majjeem, care to take us back to the top?" I asked.

"Oh, I would love to do that," she replied.

Majjeem opened the doorway, and soon all of us were walking out to the open area most of us feel is the city park.

As we walked out, my mom looked at Majjeem and said, "You got the hang of that."

"I think I have, but it's like they say, science and power, moving of the molecules and space can create an opening," Majjeem replied.

Mom joined our other mothers as they greeted our new arrivals. Then came all the introductions. Mom introduced George and April to everyone, and of course, there was lots of talk going on.

Stepping up in front of many of the people here, I spoke out, saying, "We had planned on gathering everyone and talking about moving on."

One of Nomi's crew asked, "How soon do you plan on doing that?"

"I was planning on having everyone tell us if they wanted to stay here, go home, or travel on to Palindrome with us. However, I feel we need to set up a few things here to make sure all these people are safe," I disclosed.

"When do you plan on traveling west?" Nomi asked.

"Sometime soon, I hope. But that depends on a few new problems now. Before, it seemed like a simple pack-up and move-on situation, but now I see we need to have a person here who can get those trees moved, open doorways, along with making sure those logs get to the mill."

Nomi spoke out, saying, "Marty, I'm not sure anyone but you or Steve can move all those logs down there safely."

Steve commented, "That's what he is getting at."

Soon all of us were together and talking about what we had planned for the next few days. Many of Nomi's men wanted to move on to find out about the crew no one heard from for over a year. Then a few wanted to get to that next small group of people, as they had relatives there.

I said, "Let's see who wants to remain here or travel with us and who wishes to return home."

Jack said, "We need to find out if there truly is a problem out west, as we have not run into any huge bugs with wings or firestorms, and I am sure if Marty felt them, he would say so."

"Very true, Jack," I replied.

Bailey spoke out, saying, "We will have to have a way for all those trees down below to be pulled off the top, trimmed, then sent to the mill."

Anthony spoke out, saying, "All we need is a safe way to get the trees off the pile because once they are on the ground and spread out, then people will trim them. Then maybe your parents or someone can open a doorway to the mill, and we can move all the logs."

I looked at Anthony and said, "We need to travel forward and see if whatever everyone ran from is still around. We need to go all the way to Palindrome to be sure."

"I understand," he replied.

Soon, Tony and Nomi climbed up on a wagon bed next to me. Nomi yelled out, "Hey, all of you please pay attention. We are trying to solve a few problems here so we can head further out west."

Everyone gathered around, and it became so silent. I spoke out, saying, "Some of us must travel farther west to find out what the problem has been for farmers and homesteaders out here."

One of the people standing in front of us asked, "You're leaving this place already?"

Nomi said, "We still must find out what caused all the problems in this region, and please keep in mind that we have not heard from the excavation crew near the giants' town site in over a year."

I said, "Yes, and we need to find out a few things. First off, if you have been traveling with us, do you wish to continue or would you rather stay here and help rebuild this city?"

One of the men stepped forward and said, "To be honest with you, if my wife would like to stay here and help rebuild the city, I would too."

A few others commented about staying to help with the rebuild. A few of them said they would stay and work for a few weeks but then had to return home.

"OK, all of you need to figure out what you want to do. Travel with Marty and all of them, return home, or stay here," Anthony said.

Several people were now coming over and asking, "How soon will you be moving farther west?"

I replied, "As soon as we have a way to protect all the people here and down below as they cut and remove trees."

Bailey commented, "There are a number of people still down below who said they would like to stay here. So, I told them one of us would get back to them later or in the morning to find out what they wish to do."

I was getting a feeling of excited people, and I turned to see a small group of about twelve people joining us, with one of them saying, "We have found a perfect place for a huge garden to grow food here. It's a massive building that still has walls but a solid floor that has about a foot of dirt on it."

One of the other people stated, "We are farmers and gardeners, and to us, this is a true treasure."

"We need to return to Etheral and get seeds, and planting starts because the soil in that building is perfect for planting," one woman said.

"We may have some returning to Etheral shortly, so you can get what you need for plants at that time. Will that work for you?" I asked.

"Oh, yes," was the reply.

CHAPTER 32

Pterodactyl

"I feel until we can make sure everyone here is safe, and if it takes another day or two, so be it," I shouted.

Nomi and the others nodded their heads in agreement.

Anthony spoke out one more time, saying, "If any of my group wishes to return home at any time while this group or their parents are here, I am sure they will be willing to open up a way home. At least I hope so." Then as he added that, he looked at me and kind of shifted his weight to one side and grinned.

I spoke out, saying, "Our parents will be here for some time, and if you need to return home, they will take care of you."

All at once, I got a feeling of hunger, and it was not from the people in this crowd.

Jasmin, are you and your mother flying around? I asked.

We are in a field, Marty, as we are visiting with old friends. Do you need us for something? she asked.

Marty? she asked again.

Steve reached over and tapped me on the shoulder, saying, "Hey what's going on?"

I was still trying to figure out what it was I was I felt.

Bailey looked at Steve and then at me, asking, "Marty, hello, earth to Marty."

Steve yelled, "Marty," and I turned to him and said, "Move everyone undercover now and round up anyone with powers."

"What?" he asked.

"Steve, we are going to be attacked very soon, and we must make sure everyone finds a place where they can get inside or undercover now," I said.

I was thinking how Jasmin was trying to say something about visiting friends, and I didn't get that last part. However, I noticed my father and yelled, "Dad, we need everyone rounded up from Etheral and the mill who are up here and taken down below where doors can be opened to Lower Etheral and the mill now—no wagons, but people and animals. We are about to be attacked."

Suddenly an opening was created, and people from up here were entering and walking out down below to meet up with others who would soon be leaving for safety. Within a few minutes of everyone stepping out of the doorway down below, two doorways were opening again for people heading back to the mill and Lower Etheral.

Steve was yelling at everyone, "Find shelter, a place to hide, or a building to be safe in as we are about to be attacked."

Anthony and Mortice ran up just as Steve asked me, "Where is this attack coming from?"

"The sky. Do you remember those flying reptiles we had to kill at the palace?"

"I do," he replied.

"Flying reptiles?" Anthony asked.

"In our world, they are long gone, but not here," Steve said.

"Well, it seems we have about thirty or more of them headed our way," I replied.

"Nomi, we need to get all the people and their animals at this site to a safe area. I would suggest the tunnel through the mountain. Please get whatever weapons you have ready to use," I stated.

Bailey, will you please have all of those with power and all of Sophia's archers ready as we are about to be attacked by that same kind of creature that grabbed Tabby at the palace?

Marty, I'm sure a few of us can take care of one of them, she replied.

I'm sure, but there are about thirty or more heading our way now. So please yell at Art and Tom and our parents as well letting them know what's heading our way, I stated.

I will, she replied.

Jasmin, sorry I was interrupted. How far away are you? I asked.

Maybe an hour or so. What's up? she asked.

I am getting the feeling we are about to be attacked by about thirty or more of the flying bat-like creatures we had to fight off at the palace.

We will be there as soon as we can, so stay safe until we get there, she commented.

"Someone needs to run over and yell at our blacksmiths and those with them to stay inside until this is taken care of," I yelled.

John yelled back, "I will tell them."

"Stay inside with them until the danger has passed, John," Nomi yelled back.

People were heading to the castle and some of the other large buildings where we had stored supplies and things, as they were very well protected. Wagons were being rolled back into the long building, and some of them were being moved into the tunnel area, with people grabbing shovels, axes, or whatever else they could find for a weapon. Once those wagons were moved into that area, people were getting into those wagons or under them. I noticed our parents, Majjeem, Medina, and Jack there to help protect them.

Phil and Mortice had their guards ready with weapons and swords set up in the tunnel on the far side of the people and near the entrance to protect everyone.

Suddenly, Tom and Art arrived, with Tom saying, "Well, we finally get to see God at work, it seems."

I turned to him and replied, "Hey, you're the god of thunder, not me. I'm no god. I'm just a kid from Walla Walla, Washington, remember?"

Everyone around us broke out laughing, and I said, "Maybe it's time for the god of thunder to show us his stuff."

"My stuff," he asked.

"I want to see if you're as good as Thor on TV," I said.

Art looked at both of us and said, "You two children need to get ready to fight."

"All right, our group of power needs to get on the top of that large building as it's one of the best structures here," I said as I pointed to one of the taller buildings near us.

"How far away are they?" Steve asked.

"About an hour or less," I replied.

"How come you didn't feel them at a greater distance?" Mortice asked.

"I'm not sure as they were just there all at once, as if they popped out of a mountain or something," I said.

Someone yelled from the castle tower, "The sky is getting black east of us."

I turned to Anthony and asked, "All your people have returned to Etheral, correct?"

"Yes," he replied.

"Please make sure," I asked.

I took a stance with Art, Tom, Steve, and most of our team members on the roof of one of the larger buildings. Tom asked, "Do you think we need some kind of cover?"

Steve replied, "We may find it will be easier to view all of them if we are spread out here and watch each other's backs."

The attack was soon to begin. All of us on top of a large building we could now hear screams and yelling and all of us were now getting ready to use our powers.

Tom changed into Thor, hammer and all, and even Art turned into a warrior with his armor. Of course, all our pets were giving Tom the side-view look and a grin. Those who could not toss fire had brought a bow and a bundle of arrows.

As everyone changed, I did a quick look to see if people were around us who didn't know about Tom or Art. Most of those who could see us already knew about them, so my mind was now at ease, and I was ready for action too.

Tom said, "You know, I can probably blast all of them out of the sky with a massive amount of lightning."

I replied, "The only problem with that is Jasmin and Sky are on their way and you might harm them as well. Can't you do a pick-and-choose thing?"

"I can do that, as I can throw my hammer at them, taking a few of them out of the air," he replied.

Ziggy and Agatha were listening to what he said, and Ziggy asked, "Why would you throw your hammer away?"

"I thought we discussed this already, little ones. It always comes back," he replied.

"What if your hammer doesn't come back?" Agatha asked.

He looked at the two of them and asked, "Have you ever tried since the last time we talked about that?"

Ziggy and Agatha looked at each other, and Agatha replied, "I don't want to lose my hammer. Are you crazy?"

All of us laughed and kept looking at the sky, which seemed to be getting darker farther east.

All of us were looking at each other, and I could feel most of those with us on that roof were ready, but from all those on the ground and in hidden areas, I felt fear, lots of fear, and I could tell even Sophia and her band of archers were a bit scared, but all of them had bundles of arrows ready for the fight.

I heard Vanessa say, "Oh, dear lords, I see them and there are more than thirty of those things."

I looked down at Nomi, Mortice, Phil, Anthony, and Sophia and yelled, "All of you watch each other's backs. We see them."

I sent a thought to my mother, saying, *All of you stay safe, and if it gets worse, have one of our fathers open a door to the mill and take those who are near you through.*

We will be fine. Don't you worry. We've got this, she replied.

Then it was like a swarm of bees as if someone swatted a nest, flying straight for all of us. It was almost as if they were telling each other, it was dinnertime because they were not traveling past this mountaintop.

Tom tossed that hammer, I used my power, and Steve used the force of winds, which looked funny since they were huge ugly birds with lots of feathers and suddenly those feathers were floating to the ground and a naked bird was being blown to someplace very far away. Bailey and Vanessa were with our little warriors, and all of them were creating a fire of some kind. Max and Sam were ready to take on anything that came our way, with bows and arrows, and as a backup, they had their swords. Storm, Heather, and Krystle were making winds and tossing fire that was blowing many of them away from those below.

One of those birds made a dive and grabbed one of the kids from Sophia's group and she yelled. Tom turned and threw his hammer and nailed the creature and it dropped the kid, as he was falling, I grabbed him and returned him to Sophia.

Tom, and I looked at each other and I said, "Good toss."

He replied with, "Good catch."

Arrows were flying, weapons were being fired, and everywhere we looked in the sky, we could only see black ugly batlike creatures. But the ground was starting to turn black as well, as many of them would never attack anyone again.

Soon all of them were flying and following a few who must have been the masterminds of this destruction, but there had to be at least half of what attacked us now on the ground.

I watched as our parents, Majjeem, Medina, and Jack were taking their share of the intruders down. I was impressed they had seen all their powers grow. A few people would run out of hiding below us to any of those birds that hit the ground—they made sure they never got back up.

I got the feeling I was waiting for and looking all around, I suddenly yelled out to everyone, "Find a place to hide, now. Everyone, go to a protected area. All of you on this roof get on the ground."

Steve asked, "Are you and I going to do our thing?"

"Nope," I replied.

Then as he looked all around, he knew why. Then he yelled, "Everyone, find a place to take shelter or get flat on the ground, now."

Everyone around us on the rooftop was now looking at the two of us, and I said, "All of you lie down on this roof, now."

Everyone with us was looking at each other, and then all of us were on the roof on our stomachs.

Without warning, every person in this city was viewing dragons all around those huge black flying creatures. Not just two dragons, but a few more of them all around those batlike creatures, and the sky became a fire. Since most of them didn't seem to flap their wings a lot to fly and only glided through the air, a few of them landed on the ground and were walking around on two feet.

People from the long building and other locations were now running with the tools, shovels, or anything they could use to end them.

Tom said, "I never saw them arrive."

"I knew they were coming as I could feel them and see them," I replied.

"How could you feel them, or better yet, how could you have seen something that was not there?" Tom asked.

Steve spoke out, saying, "Unlike Marty, I could not see them as he can when they are invisible, but I noticed a distortion in the sky after he told me everyone needed to get on the ground."

Cheers were rising all over the top of the city and people were running out and hugging each other, and all I could feel was warmth and happiness. I yelled at Sky so everyone could hear, "I see you brought a few of your friends."

A voice came from the sky like the thunder of the gods as she replied, "They have always been close in case we needed help."

Dragons were landing all over, and people were rushing up to them and finding all of them could speak as well. Looking around, I counted six additional dragons and lots of happy people.

"Well, I guess we can get off this roof now and go thank our friends for showing up, but you two may wish to change," I stated as I looked at Tom and Art.

195

"Good idea," Art commented.

"Agreed," Tom stated.

Soon all of us were climbing down from the roof and looking at each other giving each other high fives and hugs.

"Well, Tom, I was pleased to see that hammer in action. And, Art, I am not sure how you could pull knives from your belt with a new one appearing within seconds."

Art replied, "That is one of my ways of protecting myself, and today it worked to help others."

"So when one of those knives hit one of those birds, I noticed those creatures vanished. Where did they go?" I asked.

"They simply find out what space is," he replied.

Ziggy and Agatha had walked over by Tom and were looking up at him, with Ziggy asking, "Do you think our hammers can return as yours did?"

Tom turned his head and looked down at Ziggy and replied, "You do realize there is only one way to find out."

Ziggy and Agatha both looked at each other and shook their heads, with Agatha asking Tom, "Can you throw it close and have it come back?"

"I can throw it any distance and it will return, little one," he replied.

Suddenly, Ziggy and Agatha looked at each other, and Ziggy said to her, "Care to go for a walk?"

Soon both were walking off to throw their hammers.

Tom, said, "If you toss it make sure your hand is up and ready to catch it."

Both Ziggy and Agatha turned and yelled, "We will."

Chapter 33

Back to Normal

"Sky, thank you, from all of us to all of you and your friends," I said.

"We all need to celebrate the feeling of happiness and new friends," Bailey said.

And as she finished saying that, Steve said, "Sky, we don't have much here for food for all of you."

"We were eating as Marty contacted us, so we are good. I think one thing we need is time flying with our friends," she stated.

I looked over and said to her, "Please tell your friends they will always be safe around all of us. So fly safe and locate a place to get some sleep, up here or down below."

"We will fly and locate a place and sleep, but be sure you keep us up to date on anything you may need help with," she replied.

"You and I will have to talk about how your friends have been with us all this time and I never knew that," I spoke.

"We will do that soon, my friend," she said.

Soon dragons were standing and flapping their wings and were suddenly gone. Tom and Art walked over, with Art saying, "That was amazing, and I still don't understand how all of you can do most of the things you do."

"Everything has come with time and we can discuss it all later," I stated.

"I guess we can," Art replied.

"Well, I guess we need to get back to figuring out how to move west again," Nomi commented.

"I guess so," I replied.

Steve asked, "You don't feel any more of those flying-bat cave creatures, do you?"

I replied, "No, Robin," and then we laughed.

I looked around to see if I could find Zane and asked my father, "Have you seen Zane lately?"

"Magness, Zane, and a few others were working on that water system the last time I saw him," Dad replied.

"Dad, would you please bring our people back from the mill and Lower Etheral."

"I will see about that and make sure no one is hurt here."

Art, Tom, and Steve were walking over toward me, and I waited until they arrived and said, "We need to locate Zane and see if we can set up some ground rules, a city guild lines, and even a mayor of some kind."

Tom replied, "That would be helpful if this city is to get back to being an actual township again."

Strolling over to the building that housed the boilers and pipes, we talked about several things that could be wrong in the western region. Tom was saying, "You realize what you are looking for may not be of this world, and it may be the biggest reason the two of us originally came here."

Steve asked, "What do you mean?"

Art spoke out, saying, "What he is saying is something from another universe or another world could be on this planet, causing the problems."

I said, "You realize how far-fetched that sounds? I mean aliens from another world on this planet."

Steve looked at me and said, "Seems I said something like that a while back, and you reminded me we are from another world."

"Yes, I guess I did say that didn't I?" I replied.

Thinking about that, I guess I kept thinking of this place as home in a manner of speaking, as it sure seemed like we belonged here. I asked Tom and Art, "Why would something or someone from another world want to upset what is here?"

"I don't know if that is the case, but I'm saying it could be possible," Tom replied.

Reaching the building where most of the water seemed to be heated when used, we entered and listened to see which direction we needed to head. We took the ladder down and entered the one tunnel we felt Zane and Magness were in, checking out the water lines. As we approached them, we heard Zane saying, "I'm not sure how long that fix will last. Maybe we should shut off the water to this line back at the start of this tunnel and get a few people down here to do the repair work."

Magness said, "That might be a good idea no matter what because if this line breaks, it will flood this entire level. So now that we have this patched. Let's go shut this line off just to be on the safe side."

"Sounds like you two have all this under control," I said.

All of us started laughing, and suddenly the section they had been working on blew apart, and water was now flowing.

Steve said, "I don't think I can fix this one."

Tom said, "I think you spoke too soon, Marty."

I started walking to that section of pipe, and I looked at it, saying, "I believe I heard you say there is a valve we can run back to that will shut this line off, so I think one of us needs to see how fast that valve can be shut off."

All of us ran back to the entrance of this tunnel, and Zane got to the valve first and started shutting down the flow of water. After all of us walked back down that way, we verified the water was off, and Zane commented, "I'm guessing these water lines are all like that."

"I am surprised any of them hold water," Art replied.

It was not like pipes we see back home made of metal, steel, or PVC as it was some metal fragments mixed with what looked like concrete, so I was at a loss as to how to fix it. So I said, "Now this is shut off and after it's dried out, I think we should have our fathers look at this and see what they recommend. They may have a few ideas we have not thought of yet."

The water stopped flowing, but as the five of us walked out of that tunnel, all of us were standing near the other passageways and looking in each direction.

Zane was telling us, "People walked through these tunnels, checking for problems. However, if they overlooked that one area, maybe there are more. We have to keep in mind that section of pipe that failed needs to be fixed so we can have water to that main building and the bath areas."

"These other areas don't have water running in them at this time, correct?" Steve asked.

"You're right, Steve, as there is no reason to have water flowing to places where homes and buildings have fallen or been overgrown with plants over the centuries," Zane replied.

Art suggested, "Maybe as the girls copy all those papers upstairs, we will be able to locate a few locations where we can open up a valve and allow the water to run."

Zane said, "That is a possibility, and we would just have to make sure any other place along the way had the water shut off."

"Well, I guess we should go back and let others know those baths won't be happening right away," Magness commented.

Walking back to the wagons and the center of town, we noticed Bailey, Anthony, Nomi, and a few of the people who joined us from Etheral, who seemed to be discussing something, so we walked over and joined them to see what was happening. First, I could feel the excitement from a number of them as we approached them. Then as we got closer, I could hear what it was they were tossing back and forth.

No. No one was tossing dirt, rocks, or branches. When I said they were tossing something back and forth, I referred to the words they were saying.

"Hey, what's going on?" Steve asked.

"Some of the people from Etheral want to know if they decide to travel farther out if they can join us if we can take them home later. Others want to know, if they wish to stay here, can we open the door so they can return home and get things?" Nomi asked.

"I told them that as far as I was concerned, we could do both of those things. But it will be up to all involved, and I would say that Marty, Steve, and Zane can tell us more," Bailey stated.

"Zane, what do you think?" Nomi asked.

"Well, as Carter and I have both commented about that, we feel this city needs to have a breath of new life, and I feel all of you have already started to give it that new life. So if people wish to live here, let them come," Zane said.

Our mothers came over and had been listening to what had been said, with Wanda speaking out, asking, "Will we have good warm or hot water soon?"

Magness commented, "I know all of you ladies wanted a nice warm bath, but as of now, we had to shut off the water to the main building until we can repair the water lines. So in regards to the water, I must say as of now, we must heat the water and baths as we have been doing."

"Does this mean we must travel back to get water and fill tanks and barrels until that water line is fixed?" Mom asked.

Tom spoke out, saying, "It may mean we must get water from someplace other than here at this time, but all of us now know we have good water in this city. It's just a matter of flowing water through a good water line to that one faucet."

"I believe you're correct, Tom, but right now until we do that, people will need water up here and down below. We can go and get water in the tanks of our wagons and containers. I think if anyone knows where that one good faucet or valve could be, it may be Zane or Carter. But we also now have drawings being copied that show us where all those water lines go," I stated.

"Well, it seems we need to travel for good water at this time and people want seeds and furnishings. So, Nomi, would you please round up Mortice, Tasha, Meesha, Jack, and Burdock and have them join us by the wagons?" Steve asked.

"It sounds like many of these people are going to be very happy soon, and yes, I will round them up, and we will meet you at the wagons," Nomi replied.

CHAPTER 34

Back to Where We Were

Many of us were now walking over to the wagons to speak to those who might wish to hitch up the horses and handle the teams so we could travel a short distance for good, safe water.

Tasha and Meesha, Jack and Burdock were standing near the wagons and talking about what a great place this could be. As we walked up, they turned, and Meesha asked, "Hey, what's up?"

"Rather than open a door and haul buckets of water to the wagons, I think we need to let the horses know we have not forgotten them. We need to hitch them up to the coaches and a few new wagons we found in that big shed and get ready to move to a location that has good water," I replied.

Mortice and his men were standing there listening, and one of his men asked, "Have you figured out where we will go?"

Jack spoke, asking, "We know the water is good at that location where we lost Steve. How about that place?"

Mortice replied, "That is one place with good water that is not contaminated—that's for sure."

All at once, it seemed many others were listening, and one more person added, "I know a great place to get all the water we want and it will be easier to fill the tanks, and I would be willing to bet we could see old friends and maybe even get a great meal."

All of us turned to see an enormous smile on the face of Phillip Danassia as he was nodding his head and smiling at everyone.

Mortice started laughing and said, "Who better to have than one of our own who just happens to be a captain of the guards and understands where water flows fast, old friends are nearby, and the food is always great."

Everyone broke out laughing, and George spoke up, saying, "It would give me more time to chat with the shop people about their coaches."

Magness commented, "Hey, it would be good to see those in the shop as well to see what kind of things they are making. I will have to yell at Staggerus."

Mom said, "My mother has been telling us all kinds of good things about the people she has been healing there."

Bailey added, "If we are going to Etheral, we can take those who are considering moving out here a chance to bring things back."

"I feel you won't want an entire lot of people here with you, but it would be nice if Carter and I could visit again with the king and queen," Zane interjected.

"I guess we should collect all those who wish to return to Etheral for plant seeds, furnishings, and such, or those who simply want to go home, and all the members of our crew as well. Oh and, Zane, I do figure you two are now part of our group."

"Well, let's get the horses and gather our people and those heading back to Etheral," Burdock stated.

And with that, people vanished in different directions. Steve asked, "Shouldn't we open a door to below and bring those people up here who wish to return as well?"

"That's a good idea, and then all of us can leave from here and return to this location," I commented.

With that being said, Steve replied, "I will get them."

Soon a door was opening below. Horses were hitched up, and people from Etheral were getting ready to head home and get the things they wanted to bring back.

Everyone was talking about what they needed and what they had to do. I noticed many who were wondering what we were doing and viewed Nomi walking around and speaking to all of them, telling them we were going to get safe water and take a few people back to Etheral.

Soon a door opened, and Steve along with others walked through to join us. Our team members, our new friends, and all those returning home to Etheral were now all gathered, so I asked, "Vanessa, care to do the honors?"

Suddenly, I felt a blast of great excitement as Vanessa replied, "I can do that."

"Let's open the door to the lower town area we normally leave and return to first," I said.

The doorway was created, with all of us and our wagons entering Lower Etheral. People from this town were talking about all the things they needed to bring back with them when they returned. Others were simply happy to be home.

"All of you who need to return to Upper Etheral remain with us, and those from here who plan on going back with us, be in this location tomorrow morning before noontime," Nomi yelled.

People headed in various directions to their homes. Finally, Steve saw Nomi walking away and asked, "Are you going to join us above?"

"I would love to join all of you. However, I have a family I need to see as it's always too much time away, I'm afraid. When I return home, I often wonder if they think I'm a stranger."

Steve replied, "I can understand that one. Have a good time, and see you tomorrow."

"So, the rest of you are going with us to Upper Etheral, is that correct?" Bailey asked.

"Yes, we need to do some shopping for seeds and extra tools we don't have. We will need room on one of your wagons for some of our farm items if that's okay."

"We will do whatever we need to make sure your items return with you," I replied.

"Thank you, Bailey," one of the women said.

"Vanessa, how about outside the palace gates?" I asked.

The doorway opened outside the gates of the palace. Everyone and our wagons passed through the opening. Many of the townspeople headed one way, and our team was now waiting for the guards to recognize us.

"Good job, Vanessa," Steve said.

"Well, thank you, sir," was her reply.

Bailey and I looked over at the two of them and just smiled.

The gates began to open. As they did, Mortice and Phil were both there to meet many of the soldiers from their commands. "Welcome back, sir," one of the men said.

"Thank you, Jose, it's good to be home for a while," Phil replied.

One of Mortice's men said, "You look like you have been working out, my friend."

"Oh, Marco, you know what a rough life we live." Then both of them started to laugh.

The guards were saying, "Come on, let's get you inside. Come on." And soon we were asking them where we needed to go to load up the water barrels and tanks. One of them said, "Captain, we added a new location for water, and it may be better for filling up the tanks on the wagons. If you wish to follow me, I will lead the way."

"Thank you, Donnie," Phil replied.

As Phil walked away, many of us walked over to a section of the garage area. It was the location of the other wagons and carriages. George walked over and started talking with the workers who had helped create the other fancy carriages.

George said, "I have a few ideas that may make these transporters safer and more useful. Being around them in the actual field and seeing how they handle traveling across the country, many of us have a few ideas we would love to pass by you for your consideration."

One of the men spoke out, saying, "That would be great as we have never taken one of these out and traveled very far in them. Most times, we ride them down the hill and around the outside of the walls along a few cart paths. But that's about it."

As I listened to George's conversation, I was feeling the king and some of his guards as they were heading our way. It wasn't long before we had the company of the king, and without looking up or at him, I asked, "How have you been?"

Haskin looked around and found no people other than him and his guards, so he replied, "I have been well, and how about all of you?"

Steve spoke, saying, "We have been doing well other than being attacked by about fifty of those batlike creatures that attacked us here some time back."

"You were attacked?" the king asked.

"Yes," I replied.

"Is everyone well?" he asked.

"Everyone is fine, and our dragons came to our rescue with a few other dragons. But now we need to load up on good clean water. Unfortunately, we have been running low on that since the water system in the city still needs repairs."

Haskin remarked, "It must be difficult not having running water over there."

Tasha commented, "We have good people working on it, and they should have it fixed soon. Most of us are looking forward to a nice warm bath."

The king laughed and said, "Tasha, you can all get a good warm bath here while everyone is loading things up and after getting a good meal."

"Thank you, Your Majesty, both of those sound fantastic," Tasha replied.

"If she gets in a bathtub, she will probably never get out," Meesha said.

"Well, I'm sure I will want to get out when the water gets cold," Tasha replied.

The king was looking around and said, "Please excuse me for a few minutes, I will be right back." Haskin walked over to Phil and spoke to him briefly and returned.

Everyone was talking about the city and what we had been doing with the trees. I commented to Haskin, "It looks like we may have a large load of lumber for homes in that mountain city, this city here, our base camp, and plenty of wood for new wagons and carriages."

Haskin replied, "That will be wonderful, and I will pay you so you can reward all the people who are helping to make that happen."

"Thank you, Your Majesty," I replied.

As we were speaking, I received a few words from Gram, and said, "Excuse me for a moment, Your Majesty, seems my grandmother is talking in my head." Then we both laughed.

Marty, I can feel you here. However, I have never shown you my clinic. Will you have time to view it? Gram asked.

Gram, I'm speaking with the king at the moment. Please let me get back to you, I stated.

That will be fine if I can see you before you run off again and show you my doctor's office, she replied.

Looking forward to seeing it, Gram, I replied.

Well, it's kind of like my own home with an enlarged area for an office and a few rooms for exams. And I even have a few who help me take care of patients.

That's amazing, so now you are Dr. Fix It, I replied.

I guess so. Anyway, I want to see you before you leave. I enjoyed being out in that city with all of you before, but I felt I am needed here, she added.

I will see you before I leave, Gram, and maybe see your doctor's office. But now I need to speak to the king, I replied.

As I finished speaking with Gram, the king was telling me, "After all of you arrived and told me you were heading out west that first time, one of my staff stated that a large water wagon could be a good idea for people way out in that desolate area. So I asked him if he had an idea or design in mind and, if so, if he would care to speak to the members of our shop."

"So did he have an idea that was good?" I asked.

"He came up with a few different ideas, and the shop members showed me some drawings that looked like they would work. After a few days, I walked out to the shop, and they had already started to create it. Come with me," Haskin said. I followed Haskin over to the backside of the wagon shed. As we walked around the corner of the building, we saw Phil, and the king asked him, "Would you like to show Marty what we have been working on?"

"Yes, Your Majesty," he replied. Then the king and I followed Phil to another building, where he opened the double doors, and in front of us was another wagon. As we walked around it, I noticed a large hose that was coming from a very large valve at the top of the box in the back of this wagon.

Phil said it should be almost full, so he jumped up on the back of the wagon and was looking inside where the hose was placed. After a few minutes, Phil yelled to me, "Marty, please turn that valve off."

I walked over and started turning the valve off. Finally, Phil handed me the hose and asked me, "Would you hang this up on that hook, please?" And he was pointing to one on the wall.

Haskin said, "It looks like you're ready to go, Marty, with a full tank of clean fresh water."

"This is amazing, sir. And, Phil, you knew about this all the time?" I asked.

"I knew it was being built but didn't know it was done until I was asked to fill the tank a while ago," he replied.

Haskin spoke out, saying, "I knew sooner or later this would be needed out west. However, when all of you returned and spoke of contaminated water, I felt we had to create it. So now is as good a time as any to give it a try, so I will have someone bring horses over here in the morning, then you and Phil can take this with you."

"Sir, I am not sure what to say other than 'thank you.' This truly will be one thing we will need where we are, and probably where we will be going."

"I'm just happy we have the means and the people to create things like this for you," he replied.

CHAPTER 35

Getting Things in Order

Phil and I walked out of the shed with Haskin to join the others who were filling two coaches' water tanks. Phil asked, "Shouldn't we tell them and show them?"

Haskin said, "Now might be a good time, Marty."

"Oh, not yet, my friends, we will make them think this is all the water they will be getting this time. But before we head back, Phil and I will pull that new water wagon out and surprise them all."

Haskin looked at me and said, "Steve told me you loved the word *sandbagging*."

We looked at each other and started laughing.

Haskin called out, saying, "We have dinner being created, my friends, and all of you are invited to join us."

Everyone had a great dinner, a hot bath, and a good night's sleep. In the morning, a great breakfast was enjoyed, and as everyone was chatting and discussing things that needed to be taken back, I said, "I need to find my grandmother and see her office."

Phil said, "Let me show you where it is, my friend," and we walked out the front gate. About three blocks away, I viewed a building that had a sign on the front that read, "Doctor's Office."

I entered the building and there was Gram, so I asked, "Is the doctor in?"

We both laughed and Phil joined in.

Gram said, "Hey you, I just wanted to say I love you and want you to stay safe. I didn't have a chance to speak with you out there in the city while I was there, but I did have the time to visit with your mother and father again."

She showed us the clinic, and we said our goodbyes. Phil and I were on our way back to the group that was waiting for us.

Everyone was now milling around the wagons just outside the open gates to the palace, and as I walked up, Bailey asked, "Do you want an opening to Lower Etheral?"

"Do we have everyone with us and we're not forgetting anyone?" I asked.

Everyone was looking around to make sure all their friends were with us and then people started saying things like "We're all here."

So Bailey asked me again, "Do you want a door to Lower Etheral?"

I looked over at Phil and winked then turned back to Bailey and said, "Not just yet, as we have one more wagon going with us."

Phil and I had already had horses set up on the wagon and one of his guards in the seat, and as I spoke, Phil walked over by the gate and waved. Suddenly a new larger wagon with wider wheels came rolling out of the gates.

Everyone turned and walked over and was asking the guard in the seat, "What kind of wagon is this?"

As Phil and I walked up, the guard stated, "This is a brand-new water wagon to be used out west."

Everyone was walking around it and looking up at it, as the entire tank was sitting on a flat surface with braces along the sides and six large straps running over it to the other side, and it was probably about eight feet in length and around five feet tall.

As Bailey walked over, I felt her headed my way, then she bumped into me as if it was an accident, saying, "Keeping secrets, are we?"

"No, Bailey, just a surprise. So now you can open that doorway if you wish."

Soon all of us were walking out in Lower Etheral, meeting Nomi, surrounded by people. As we pulled up, I asked Nomi, "Do we have everyone?"

He replied, "We do, and it looks like you have another new wagon."

I responded, "We do, and it's full of water."

"I guess someone must have been thinking of us," he countered.

"I think the king knew sooner or later we would need it," I commented.

I climbed up into the back of one of the larger wagons. I looked all around at everyone here to see if we had all those who wanted seeds, those who needed items from homes, and anyone else who needed supplies. I felt everyone was with us, so I asked, "Who cares to open the door to the city on the mountain?"

Vanessa said, "I can do it, especially since I can now open one larger than a foot around." Then it happened.

Arriving back in the city, everyone was fascinated as two regular wagons rolled out with gardeners, home furnishings, and supplies and they were followed by our two coaches. But it was that last wagon behind those two coaches that got their attention.

People were so interested in that last wagon they forgot they wanted water. But soon Bailey yelled out, "Okay, everyone who has buckets or containers they wish to fill with water, grab them and come back here. This is our new water wagon."

As people were filling up with water, Steve opened a door below, and Anthony and all of them came up and filled all their containers. Then after about half an hour, Steve opened another door for them to return.

Looking around, I viewed many of those flying batlike creatures' bodies and I asked George and my father, "Remember Emmitt Bastion, the bird guy?"

Dad replied, "Of course, as we often stopped to visit with him whenever we would head to town."

George said, "Yes of course, why do you ask?" he questioned.

I looked at both as I was looking around the ground, saying, "I think we have one he does not have."

Dad asked, "Did you want to take one of these to him?"

"Yes," I replied.

"Great idea, Marty, let me get a tarp or something to put one of these on, and we will join you," George replied.

Soon, George, Dad, and I were stepping out on the pathway of Emmitt's property. We looked around, and I said, "I do hope he's here as I don't want to just drop it off and leave."

Both my father and George were looking around and suddenly felt him behind us and then heard, "Well, well, well, what do we have here?"

Turning around, we viewed Emmitt walking out of this huge barn area where he studied all the different kinds of birds. George said, "Emmitt, you remember Fred and Marty?"

"Oh, but of course," he replied.

"Marty wanted to bring you a gift from about twenty days away from here," my father was saying as he was opening a tarp with one of the creatures from the attack.

"Oh my, I have heard of those but never seen one in my entire life. Is this for me to study?" he asked.

"I knew you need one more bird to study, my friend, and this one is only one of the many that attacked us. However, we must return to a city on top of a mountain in the western Denarian region," I answered.

"How did you get here and how long have you been traveling? Are you hungry? Where is your wagon?" he asked as he was looking all around.

George asked me, "Can he come back with us for a day or two?"

I looked at Emmitt and said, "Please shut all your doors and windows, and make sure your birds have food and water. We're going for a walk."

When the door to the center of the mountaintop city had opened, Emmitt was looking all around with his mouth wide open, leaning over past the opening and looking at everyone and everything. As I held the opening, George walked up to him, grabbed his arm, Dad grabbed the other, and all four of us stepped out of that opening. April and Vanessa saw us and ran over to hug him, and even as he was getting hugs, he was still in a daze-like state, looking around with his mouth still open.

Many others were now joining us, and soon all our team members were bending his ear.

No, no one was bending anyone's ear with their hands or anything else. They were talking to him.

I said, "Emmitt, we have things that must be done, so I will now leave you to wander around and learn. Oh, and if you noticed, there are a lot more of those flying lizards scattered around this city."

Suddenly he found himself telling the children all about birds. As the kids and others were learning more about those batlike creatures from Emmitt, George and I turned to see my father walk up with Robert and Mark.

Robert said, "If you wish to head out west, we will open the doors from here to below and from there to the camp, and if needed, we can open them to the palace or Lower Etheral as well if that will help."

"Well, that will take care of the openings, but now we still have to make sure those people are not hurt or killed trying to move those trees," I replied.

My father said, "Well, for now, the three of us are going to round up Zane and Magness and head over to that water house to see what we can figure out with those pipes."

"That would be good, catch you all later," I replied.

Phil and Mortice approached me, and Mortice asked, "Do you have any answer to how those down below can move those trees safely?"

"No, I don't yet, but I keep getting the feeling if we get everyone out of the way, Steve and I could see about applying wind and strength to that pile and spreading them out enough that people could get in and around them safely."

I sent a thought to Steve: *Where are you now?*

Just talking with Vanessa. What do you need? he asked.

I was thinking we should get people out of the way down below and use our powers to spread all those trees out, removing them from that huge pile.

Steve answered, *That may be the best way to handle that situation. When do you want to do that?*

I think the sooner the better, as our fathers said they can open the doors while we are gone.

I will meet you in the park area, Steve stated.

I will be there, I replied.

"I have one idea of how to make sure all those people can work on those trees without getting hurt or killed," I stated.

Steve said, "What you suggested may be the best thing that can happen, but we should have someone up on that view area looking down to tell us if there are areas that need to be blown apart or moved even more."

I looked around and noticed Jack and Burdock close by, and we presented them with our idea.

Jack spoke out, saying, "We can go out there, but we won't be able to communicate with you. So how about having Bailey or Vanessa join us?"

I looked around and noticed both and asked Bailey, *Can you and Vanessa join us, please?*

Be right there, she replied.

After explaining what we had in mind, the four of them headed to the viewpoint, and Steve and I walked through an opening I created.

"Tony, we would like you to round up all your people down here. We need to move all your camp and wagons over by where Jasmin and Sky were sleeping if you would, please," I stated.

"What's going on?" he asked.

"We have an idea of how to spread out more of these trees, but we need all your people behind us," I declared.

"It will take a few minutes to make sure I can get all of them to pay attention and then move them," he disclosed.

We waited around for a good amount of time, and suddenly I heard, *We are here and will be watching.*

OK, Bailey, still waiting for Tony to get all his people to a safe place. Let me know if you see any stragglers, please.

Will do.

I turned to Steve and said, "They are ready up topside."

"That's good," Steve replied.

Vanessa sent, *We are looking, and none of us see any people being left behind at this time.*

Good, just waiting for Tony now to make sure all his people are safe. I see them moving a wagon now, so it should not be much longer.

"Whatever you plan on doing, I feel all the people are now behind all of us with the wagons and camp gear," Tony exclaimed.

Can you see us where we are now? If so, can you tell me if we blow the trees away from us, does that look like it would help even things out? I asked Bailey.

If you blow those trees away from you, that will help to even things out, but you may wish to shake them to get some of that dirt off them, she answered.

"Alright, if I raise trees, Bailey thinks we need to shake and rock them to dump off the dirt. I will try to do that, then you can blow them to the other side of that pile. She said that may even things out more. What do you think? Are you ready for this?" I asked.

"I guess if you pick them up and drop them then pick them up again, I can blow wind on them that may remove some of that dirt, and if some blow to the other side, it won't hurt," he disclosed.

So I started picking trees up, shaking them, and Steve used his wind. After moving a good number to the other side of that pile, I started bringing them toward us, shaking and dropping them, then picking them back up. After I did that, I started backing up and dropping them next to each other. We still had a huge pile in the center, but now, Anthony and his men joined Steve and me as we walked around and looked at both sides of that huge pile. We were viewing hundreds of trees spread out and not piled on top of one another.

I asked Anthony, "Will your people be able to work on all these safely?"

He turned and looked at the people with us, and almost all of them were nodding their heads yes.

Steve and I looked at all those trees one more time. It looked a lot safer than what we saw before. So I turned to Anthony and said, "Tony, do not work on that huge pile of trees, have your people only work on the ones that are safe."

"I will make sure everyone trims only the ones we see spread out now," he replied.

"When you need more pulled down, you have one of our fathers let me know, and Steve and I will return. Our fathers are going to open the doorways for you to the mill, up on the hill and Etheral. If you have problems, have our fathers contact us."

"I will make sure we don't have any problems if I can avoid them," Tony disclosed.

"Additionally, whatever you trim off the trees we need to cut for firewood and move to one location in the city. It might be good to have a wagon you can load up with firewood. I will have someone find a good location for that. Any questions you have, you should ask them now because I feel we will be on the road again in the morning."

"I think right now all our people are going to examine the different locations of trees to figure out where they will be working tomorrow. Now we will have to rearrange our campsite, but I feel this may work well. So you're going to be traveling west again? Is that correct?" he asked.

"Yes, it looks like we have a good amount of help up in the city, with Zane and Carter helping them. It looks like you have plenty of help down here, but if you need more, ask our fathers for it. And all of you stay safe," I said.

"I will have your father contact you when it looks like we will need more trees, so until then, both of you be safe, my friends, and see both of you again soon," he declared.

Looks like we are done here, so meet you back at the open area, I sent to Bailey.

Okay, see you both soon, she answered.

"Care to do the honors?" I asked.

"I guess since you just asked that, this must be a ceremonial function we take part in," Steve said.

I looked at him and slightly turned my head, tipped it down laughing, and backed up slowly, and as I said, "It is, my friend," I was nodding my head.

CHAPTER 36

Getting Ready to Ride

When we arrived back in the city, we were met by members of our team asking questions about whether it was safe for all those people.

Steve commented, "It's now a lot safer than it was before we went down there. And Tony knows to have our fathers contact us if they need help."

"I feel we have things in order, so we can all move further west now," I stated.

"Now that is good news," Burdock said.

Vanessa said, "Marty, my father said you took Emmitt a gift, but I think the real gift was bringing him back here because he can now teach kids about birds."

"Well, he can, but he will not want to leave his home for any great length of time as he has birds there as well. So we must figure out some way he can visit here and teach and return home," I stated.

"Vanessa, please be sure all of our fathers have a view of his home so one of them can return him when he's ready to go back."

"I will, Marty, but I'm sure he won't want to go back soon," she stated.

Finding Nomi and a few others, I asked, "Will you be ready to ride out in the morning to head west?"

"Marty, I've been ready to ride out west for a few days." Then he started laughing and we joined in. "But do we have everything squared away to keep people safe?"

"Steve and I have both given a thought about the safety of everyone with all the events we have seen lately. I feel if there is trouble, we are a message away."

"I think with Zane up here along with our fathers, for communication purposes, we will know if they need help of any kind. So I would have to say it's time to rock and roll," I added.

Mortice spoke, asking, "So we leave in the morning?"

"We do, my friend," Nomi replied.

Yes, it was time to move on as we had done all we could at this location, however new information, facts and understanding still awaited us.

With all our travels into the western region, we feel now we are close to the city of the giants.

However, what we found next was a surprise none of us expected.

Please be sure to find out about
the city of Giants in

Book Seven

GLOSSARY OF PEOPLE AND EVENTS IN THE BOOKS

Imperealisity

<u>Characters from the town of Walla Walla on Earth</u>

Marty. A teenager from Earth who has powers of strength and force.

Bailey. A teenager from Earth who has the power of vision, with an invisible shield.

Steve. A teenager from Earth who has powers of strength, wind, and translation.

Mary or **Gram**. Marty's grandmother.

Marie and **Fred Daniels**. Marty's parents.

Wanda and **Mark Rogers**. Steve's parents.

Robert and **Catrina Anderson**. Bailey's parents.

Ziggy or **Princess Zamora**. Marty's pet pup.

Maximillian or **Max**. Steve's ferret, or whatever he wants to become.

Tabetha or **Tabby**. Bailey's cat.

PEOPLE FROM THE NEW WORLD

Denarian team members from Imperealisity

Denarians. What we call dwarfs back home. The name sounds like "D-nair-e-ins."

Burdock. A Denarian team member.

Datilina. A Denarian team member.

Dohadie. Burdock's brother and a street vendor.

Magic. Cook at the base camp and a Denarian team member.

Meesha. A Denarian team member.

Oscar. A Denarian team member.

Ruther. A Denarian team member.

Tasha. A Denarian team member.

Winterish. A Denarian with a companion bear named, Healer

Other people and pets from Imperealisity

Arrion. The elf prince of Adonai. The name sounds like "R-re-on."

Agatha. Vanessa's pet pig.

Anthony. Leader of the people who were bandits and soon changed. He and all his people rebuilt Old Etheral. He is the one Marty picked up and left hanging in midair for some time on the road to Etheral.

Anubis. God of the underworld.

Atherton, Sophia. A waitress from Molumphy but is now our best archer.

Averell. Elder of the towns of Etheral.

Bastion, Emmitt. The birdman with books of drawings and a building of live birds of all kinds. And he has fantastic food.

Bogarts. **Jeff** and **Susan** and their son, **Adam**. Neighbors of the Roberts.

Carter. A caster that was brought back to life

Danassia, Philip. The captain of the guard for the elders.

Day, Manna. From the town of Ledkin, she said, "I can cook." And she can.

Gaspard, Mathew. Became the lumber-mill operator at the base camp.

Haskin. The king of the towns of Etheral

Jasmin. The young dragon found on the road.

Majjeem. Enchantress of the Nicoya tribal people. The name sounds like "Ma-sheem."

Marcus. Leader of the northern tribe of Matusz, gypsies in Medina's forest

Masher. Companion and protector of Medina. A big gray wolf.

Marta. Owner of the bathhouse and laundry in Molumphy.

Mathews, Tony, and his wife, **Becky.** The store owners in Molumphy

Medina. The goddess and protector of forests and all wildlife.

Metzler, John. The excavation crew member leading the way past the gates in the fog.

Mincer. Elder of the towns of Etheral

Mortice Rebello. The captain of the guard for the king and queen of Etheral.

Natalie. The queen of the towns of Etheral

Negator Reeves. The high wizard, or as they say in this world, Wise One of the Galenian realm. He contacted Marty in an abandoned small building, in the form of a hologram asking for help when Marty and his team finished helping the Denarians.

Neeta. Majjeem's daughter.

Roberts, George and **April.** Father and mother of Vanessa, Krystle, and Heather.

Roberts, Heather. Daughter of George and April and sister of Vanessa and Krystle.

Roberts, Krystle. Daughter of George and April and sister of Vanessa and Heather.

Roberts, Marilyn. The sister of April Roberts.

Roberts, Mike. Brother-in-law of April Roberts.

Roberts, Vanessa. Daughter of George and April and sister of Krystle and Heather.

Stargazer, Jack. A Wise One or wizard was found sitting near the road in Book Two.

Sam. Krystle's cat.

Sky. Mama dragon.

Snowball. Heather's cat Snowball is now called Strom since everyone viewed her powers.

Sirbilix. A changeling who is now known as Art Newman. The name sounds like "Sir-bill-ix."

Tangent. Elder of the towns of Etheral

Tinder, Nomi. Leader of the excavation crews, he looks like a small bulldozer.

Thorborn, Thomas. The person whom everyone was waiting on to arrive said he came from a town called Denny Borrow across the sea. But as all of us found out, his real name is Thor.

Warren McDaniel. A local constable.

Zachary and his wife **Elena**. The farmers we found after facing a tornado and dealing with the flood showed us how to create a remarkable water supply.

Zane Davain. The wizard, or as they say, wise one Carter loved.

Information about words used in the books

Adonai. The home world of the elves.

Asgard or **Aesir**. Home world of Odin and the Norse gods.

Be-judos. Scaring the heck out of someone.

Bobbles Burrow. A café in Molumphy.

Cardo. Another word for dynamite.

Cartful act. Circus.

Charros. Potatoes.

Coche. An average person in the world of Imperealisity who has never seen an elf. The view from an elf.

Dataset. Has big ears, an exceptionally long fluffy tail, and stripes of black and white with a face that looks like he is always smiling.

Dedra brush. A plant that cures rashes and body mold.

Doggers. People who sit on their butt and complain or put down others.

Donnies. Air bladders are like an air mattress, only heavy-duty.

Dorga. Wild boar.

Etheral. The combination of three different towns: Old Etheral, Lower Etheral, and Upper Etheral. These are all Denarian town locations.

Gas storm. A red cloud that stays close to the ground as it's moving, smells twice as bad as the smell of a skunk.

Gazetteer. A creature that looks like a rabbit with the face of a bird with a long beak, horns, and long claws. They control the poppadum overpopulation.

Gobble bobber. A big prehistoric animal one person talked about, saying they are used to move huge rocks in the southern mountain range.

Hawkins. Llamas.

Idiopids. Creatures that look like children with the facial features of a kitten with big round eyes. They have hands and feet like a person. Small animals always look so sad until they find a mate, then they bounce around like one big furry ball.

Knockers. A game that is similar to a game of pool.

Ledkin. A village where people created homes on some of the largest trees ever seen. We visited the town on the road to Etheral.

Liquid kittling. A substance like nitroglycerine.

Mark and **Darnie** are both men on Anthony's crew.

Merkish. A saying that is like "It's all Greek to me."

Molumphy. The town where we met Tony Mathews and his wife Becky, as they owned the store in Molumphy we had to barter with.

Nappers. Spiders.

Netti rocks. These are small pieces of a rock formation that can be used by creating a spark, and they make a glow or even heat up things such as water or a campfire.

Poppadum. Creatures that must be like gophers. We never saw any of them; however, we did see lots of mounds of dirt.

Pew yews. Skunks.

Porret. A drink much like coffee.

Raniango. A very large animal that looks bigger than a horse and has horns, with lots of hair, and red eyes, spits out the juice that burns and can melt about anything including people. Oh, and it has a bad temper.

Red bird. "Redbird" is the only name we could give this one as it followed us for many hours and miles. We watched as it was being attacked and we yelled to warn it, and it was as if it knew what we were yelling as it burst into flames for protection and vanished.

Scroll. A tab or credit.

Scriptable. Money.

Smackers. A saying where something seems so great that it just comes up and smacks you between the eyes.

Smathers. Giant scorpions about three feet tall and around five feet to six feet in length surfaced and surrounded the wagons.

Starpets. Must be the same as daisies on Earth.

Tanners. Creatures that look like huge bats but are more likely to be pterodactyls.

Targus. The first beast Marty and Ziggy had to face. The beast had its head on the middle of its chest, and it was huge and green.

Tempts. Coins.

Tenkey. A word that means being upset with others because you are having a dreadful day.

Thorborn, Thomas. The person whom everyone was waiting on arrived. He said he came from a town called Denny Borrow across the sea. But as all of us found out, his real name is Thor.

Tootler. A word that describes a big lie, so I guess it would be like a whopper.

Topo. Corn.

T. rex. A dinosaur that is found in this world. This world is not like Earth as they never had the impacts that destroyed the dinosaurs as on Earth.

Trumps. Creatures that are called orcs in most other worlds. They are a clan of big, self-loving, ugly, hate-filled beasts. We caught them stealing people to use as slaves.

Twirlers. A short word for tornadoes, cyclones, or twisters.

Metathesis. One of the most destructive animals that you can find, it looks like an elk with scales, a snake's head, long sharp teeth, and it shoots out fireballs. This is the one that attacked Bailey, Marty, and our pets as Steve opened his mouth, yelling, and put it down.

Wholly crumbles. An exclamation like "My gosh!" or "Holy cow!"

Places in Washington State

Walla Walla is a historical community in southeastern Washington State: Fort Walla Walla, the meeting of Indian tribes and Lewis and Clark, the very first state governor's mansion, and so much more.

Please note that the locations in Walla Walla used in chapter 45 are real. So now you know where you can get a great pizza and a fantastic milkshake, and if you need to pick up something you need at the last moment, we even gave you the location of Goodwill.

Hanford Atomic Research Facility. Located near the tri-cities of southeastern Washington State.

Things of interest

The Blacksmiths who have joined us are Magness and Staggerus. Many people gave them the nicknames Magnum and Staggerbush, probably because of their size and the beards.

The city of the giants is called the city of greatness. However, the actual name they gave to the town was Palindrome, the fulfillment of all dreams.

Mistress Emerson. Said in place of foul words so if someone had religious beliefs, they would not be offended by a four-letter comment.

Marty's new sword. A magical sword from Masher that can change shape and let off brilliant, bright light and colors, with all the action of the gods on the side of the blade.